3/05

W

3 6817 00118021 7   W9-CFY-902

DISCARD

BUCKEYE

Center Point
Large Print

**This Large Print Book carries the
Seal of Approval of N.A.V.H.**

BUCKEYE

LAURAN PAINE

CENTER POINT PUBLISHING
THORNDIKE, MAINE

This Center Point Large Print edition
is published in the year 2001 by arrangement with
Golden West Literary Agency.

The text of this Large Print edition is unabridged.
In other aspects, this book may vary from the original
edition. Printed in Thailand. Set in 18-point Plantin type
by Bill Coskrey.

ISBN 1-58547-087-2

Library of Congress Cataloging-in-Publication Data

Paine, Lauran.
    Buckeye / Lauran Paine.
    p. cm.
    ISBN 1-58547-087-2 (lib. bdg. : alk. paper)
    1. Large type books. I. Title.

PS3566.A34 B82 2001
813'.54--dc21

00-065680

BUCKEYE

1
The Outlaw

The very early mornings were pleasant; afterwards, from about eleven o'clock onward the heat gradually increased. By mid-afternoon horses sweated just standing in the tree-shade of tie-racks and the kind of heat which lingered at Buckeye, or any other south desert community, did not abate after nightfall until past midnight. It even seemed, at times, to get hotter.

The Indians said that was because all the rocks of the south desert country stored heat all day and released it at night.

The Mexicans shrugged about that. Indians always had to work out some superstitious reason for things, usually in the form of a fairy-tale. Of course the rocks stored heat, but so did the ground and the mountains and the walls and rooftops of towns and it was all released, from every source, after sunset and onward until the stored heat equalled the coolness; then the world became pleasant again, usually about an hour or two before *dawnlight*, this lasting until about ten o'clock in the morning.

Business was briskly transacted at Buckeye before high noon. After that, most people went for their *siesta*, their nap which lasted until seven, eight, or nine o'clock. Especially in Mex-town, people commonly did not have supper until nine or ten o'clock. In *Yanqui*-town they ate earlier, heat or no heat.

That, it was commonly said, was why the outlaw had been killed after raiding the

Fort stage. The posse was armed in the saddle and in pursuit before most posses in places distant from the south desert had even got their britches on.

It was probably true. Except that what folks meant was that was probably the reason why the outlaw was *overtaken*. The reason he was *killed*, which was not the same as being run to earth, was because he tried to fight the posse. *Maybe* that was the reason.

That, said Doctor Nash, to whom they had delivered the corpse when they got back to town about dawn, tended to support a conviction of Adrian Nash's that there was no intelligent outlaws. There were sly and deadly ones, deadly and dangerous ones, vicious and brutal ones and occasionally a clever one, but no intelligent ones, or, of course, they would not be outlaws.

Turner Whitsett had been a lawman twenty-two years, the last seven of those years on the south desert at Buckeye. He was greying, russet-complexion, had light eyes and a wide mouth. He was a tall man who moved with lithe ease, smiled now and then and rarely mis-judged a man. Women, he had made mistakes about, but not men.

He had finished sluicing off up at the bath-house out behind his room at the Sullivan's hotel—which was a boarding-house, actually, the only one anywhere close to Buckeye—had re-dressed and was on his way down to the café for breakfast when Doc Nash whistled between two fingers and beckoned, so Marshal Whitsett swerved off and crossed the roadway.

Adrian Nash was a man of medium height and build and belonged to that seemingly ageless variety of men who, like their south-desert environment, just went on and on without showing their years or their disillusionments as they accumulated those years.

But he was in his sixties. He neither looked it nor acted it but he was. He had been married forty years before his wife had died. Womenfolk of course said the reason he was so well-preserved was because his late wife had taken such good care of him.

Maybe. Cynical Will Austen who owned the saloon said it was Doctor Nash's discriminatory practice of drinking nothing but very good whiskey which had preserved him. If folks had elected to make this their avocation, deciding why Doc Nash remained so youthful despite his age, they undoubtedly could have come up with another ten dozen reasons, none of which could have been proven or disproven; meanwhile Doc went along as though *he* neither knew nor cared.

When he took Marshal Whitsett on through his cottage to the back room, off the kitchen and beside the woodshed to show him the corpse of that dead outlaw, he lit a cigar and gestured with it. Anyone addicted to mellow, good tobacco could have pointed to another reason for Doc's youthfulness.

"You said he must have hid the money before you boys ran him down and cornered him. Right?"

Marshal Whitsett stood stonily gazing at the pale corpse, naked from the waist up. "That's right. According to the stage-driver he got off with the money-sack. When we got him in among the rocks, he didn't have it. And we looked high and low. Even tried to back-track him to some place where he'd cached it." Whitsett raised his pale eyes. "Why?"

Doctor Nash was not ready to answer that. "And you fellows were in front exchanging shots with him?"

"Yes . . . What are you leading up to, Doc?"

Nash pointed to a pair of purplish little puckered punctures. "One in the throat, one in the chest near the centre."

Marshal Whitsett was beginning to look annoyed. "If you mean—which one killed him—I'd guess the one in the chest. But you're the doctor and the undertaker."

Adrian Nash's handsome features slowly brightened. "Nice of you to concede that, Whit. No; that's not the bullet that killed him. Do you see any blood?"

"You washed him off," replied the township marshal, nodding in the direction of a basin with a rag in it and some pinkish water.

Doctor Nash said nothing. He leaned, propped the corpse up and heaved it over slightly onto one side. "There's the slug that killed him, Whit." He pointed with his cigar-hand to a hole almost entirely concealed in the hair at the rear of the dead outlaw's head. He looked up, eyes drawn out narrow in a shrewd expression. "You sure all the possemen were in front of him?"

"Yeah, I'm sure. We came onto him and he fired at us. We piled off and jumped into the rocks." Marshal Whitsett leaned, his

faint frown gradually deepening, but not
with annoyance now.

Doctor Nash blew smoke at the ceiling
and waited. When the law officer twisted to
glance around Doctor Nash shook his head
slowly. "He wasn't killed in front, Whit.
That's what I meant by asking if you saw
any blood on those other wounds. When a
person is dead and his heart ceases to
pump blood, he doesn't bleed. Maybe a
trickle or two, but no blood runs forth. The
heart, you see, functions as a pump to force
blood through the arteries under pressure.
When you cut yourself, for example—"

Marshal Whitsett was not listening.
"There was no one behind him, Doc.
Maybe he turned his head. There was a lot
of lead flying."

Doctor Nash turned skeptical eyes
upon his friend. "Would you turn your
head, your whole body which he would
have had to have done to get shot squarely
in the back of the head, if men were

shooting at you from in front?"

Whit drew upright and shoved big hands deep into trouser pockets, wide mouth pursed, pale eyes fixed upon the wound in the back of the dead man's skull. He stepped behind Doc to go around and look at the face. There was no exiting hole around there. Doc anticipated this and said, "The throat. The slug came out the throat, Whit."

"Then the bullet was travelling downhill. If it hit him in the back of the head like that and came out—"

"Exactly. And to me, that suggests someone was not only behind him, Whit, but also slightly above him. Now I don't know the area where he was killed—in the rocks you said—were there more rocks, or perhaps larger ones, or maybe they were on a slope?"

The marshal went back around where he had been standing. "A slope," he muttered. "Where we cornered him was just before the stageroad heads into Gregorio

Pass. It slopes a little, down there." Whitsett looked at the older man. "The gawd-damned money-pouch, Doc."

Nash turned to flip grey ash as he said, "I wondered about that." He turned back smiling. "Also wondered about something else. How much was in that money-pouch?"

Marshal Whitsett had the estimate of the stage company's local supervisor. "About nine hundred dollars. But that's a guess, Doc. The money was from Fort Hannibal on its way to the army post down at Coldspring for pay, but until the company can find out the exact amount I won't know." He sighed. "There's going to be some mad soldiers down there."

"Whit; *two* of them. How does that strike you? There were two of them. One was in the rocks behind the other one. Maybe they saw your posse coming."

"Doc, it was dark."

"All right. Then they heard you coming and got into the rocks, maybe to hide and hope you'd go past. When you didn't do that, when you cornered them, the one farther back in the rocks had a perfect opportunity to end up with all the money. . . . He shot this one and you boys assumed this was the only one, tied him on a horse and came back to town."

Whit swore briefly, but with feeling. "That's going to make us look pretty bad."

Doctor Nash did not think so. "You said it was dark. And what sticks in my craw—if that second one also knew you were coming—did he also fire at you?"

The lawman shook his head. "There was just one man firing at us, and he didn't do it all the time, just now and then, like he wasn't going to let us guess where he was hiding in those damned boulders." Whit suddenly looked up. "Yeah; it could have been two men firing. It sure didn't seem like it though and the fight was over before we got ready to work our way toward this one." Whit swore again and looked bitterly at the corpse. "I figured to go back up there with someone this morning when we got good daylight and backtrack to the cache. Doc; if there *was* another one. . . ."

Nash nodded. "No cache. Want me to *ride* back up there with you?"

Marshal Whitsett was not thinking of who would accompany him, he was thinking of how stupid he was going to look to the army, the townsmen, even the range cattlemen who would all hear about this sooner or later. He stood gazing at the corpse in dour silence until Doctor Nash set aside his cigar to ease the body back down and to cover it with a brown blanket.

"Care for some coffee?" he asked, leading the way back through to his kitchen, with its faint scent of medicine and embalming fluid.

Marshal Whitsett followed along shaking his head. Normally he would have accepted, but he had never been able to drink coffee in Doctor Nash's kitchen and he'd had many chances to do so.

The smell did not bother Adrian Nash. He filled a cup, puffed on his cigar while watching the lawman and finally said, "What the hell; something like this happens every day—somewhere."

Whit's answer was succinct. "Tell that to the army. And to folks here in Buckeye." He looked out the kitchen window into the back alley where the litter of years had been accumulating. "The darned stage-driver said one man stopped him and took the pouch and stepped back into the darkness." He swore again.

"Is that how they usually do it, Whit?"

"Well; they do it like that some time. Just as often one man lies back with his carbine backing up the one that stops the coach. That's why stage companies usually tell their gunguards to look all around first before trying to resist." He turned back to face the medical practitioner. "All the excuse I can offer is that it was dark last

night, and I had no reason to figure there'd
been two of them. Doc, an odd thing about
human nature—where money is concerned
folks aren't interested in excuses. . . . You
want to ride up there with me?"

"Sure. When?"

"Hour. I haven't had breakfast yet. I'll
meet you down at the livery barn in an hour."

They went back through to the front of
the cottage and as the rawboned, lean
lawman struck out across the road, heading
once more in the direction of the café, and
with newday light beginning to shade the
cow-town with its rarely noticed but magnificent pastels, Doctor Nash leaned in his
doorway smoking.

He rarely treated gunshot wounds;
occasionally he treated carved-up Mexicans
after a Saturday night fandango over in
Mex-town, but Buckeye was usually an
orderly place. The reason it was orderly was
just now entering the café wearing a
harassed, unhappy expression.

2

HOW TO GET A HEADACHE WITHOUT TRYING

They called Dickens Henderson "Deacon", a name his small brother had hung on him during childhood because his brother, six years old at the time, spent many a Sunday dinner with the deacon of their church as a guest, so he knew what a deacon was, and he had no idea that his mother's maiden name had been Dickens.

Deacon Henderson was in his late forties, chewed tobacco, was rough and tough and outspoken and managed the stage company's Buckeye office, depot and corralyard. When he was out front and saw Turner Whitsett and Doctor Nash riding northward in the cool, newday light, he spat, then shook his head. His stages had been stopped before, quite a number of times in fact, so it was not the robbery which bothered him; it was that this time one of his stages had lost the army payroll for Coldspring, and *that* was going to bring the army—and the main-office folks over in Deming—down on him like a load of bricks.

But when Will Austen walked up, also watching the pair of horsemen, and said, "How come if they got the outlaw last night they didn't recover the money-pouch?" Deacon Henderson offered a defense for the law. "How do you know they didn't get it? And besides, the thing ain't over with yet."

Will sniffed and struck out across the road for his place of business. He had been looking for the bad in people so long it was established habit and not even an Act of Congress would make him see much good in anyone.

Deacon was a little like that; tough and often disagreeable and uncompromising in most things, but he was not quite to the point where everyone was one of two things to him—either a bastard or a son of a bitch. Mostly they were, but not quite all of them.

He liked Turner Whitsett. It was a grudging thing but that was another facet to Deacon Henderson's character; he was a very stubborn man. If he liked someone it seemed to reflect upon him personally if they eventually did not quite measure up. But this morning he was justified and knew it; they had brought back that coach-robber in the pit of the night. Even Indians couldn't see good in the dark. He'd probably get the money bag back. Probably. He spat into roadway dust, bobbed his head with meagre gallantry as a pair of women went past on their way with shopping bags to the general store, then cast a final look up where Doc and Whit were beyond town loping northward, spat again, with particular vigour this time, and shuffled back into the corralyard.

"Damned lousy desert anyway; if it ain't rattlesnakes and gila monsters, it's outlaws!"

Marshal Whitsett felt the same way and, although he had reason to have little faith in human nature, he in fact liked most people, got along well with them and even when he had to haul them to his cell-room smoked to the gills on a Saturday night he rarely was disagreeable about it. Unless they were fighting drunks. He had been taking care of them so long he knew exactly how to do it. But they annoyed him anyway.

As for outlaws, and in this particular instance those who robbed stagecoaches in

his township, he was a silent, doggedly persevering individual with a long reputation
for rarely giving up. As he told Doctor Nash
on their pleasant morning ride, there were
too many laws on the books and not
enough penalties.

Adrian Nash was a confident, self-
assured individual with few prejudices and
no really enduring dislikes in people or
horses, or even dogs. He said, "That one
last night—he got the penalty, Whit."

The lawman grunted. "But not from
me. If it *had* been from me it wouldn't have
kept me from eating breakfast, I can tell
you that. Doc, outlaws only understand one
thing—force."

Adrian Nash was not going to get
pulled into this kind of a discussion, especially when he secretly, deep-down, agreed,
so all he said was, "Maybe we should have
brought along a tracker."

Whit had considered that over breakfast
and had done nothing about it. Now, the

closer he got to those rocks at the foot of the low pass through some thick hills northward, the more he thought daylight would be all they would need.

He was wrong. In a sense he was wrong anyway. When they got up there, to the place where blood showed, on the ground and splattered up across a big grey stone, Marshal Whitsett pointed. "Right there is where we found him dead. There—you can see our boot-tracks where we dragged him out. Now then—tie your horse Doc—and let's backtrack."

They covered less than a hundred feet. Whit stopped, staring at the ground. Doctor Nash gestured, "Where did they go?"

"Under a damn blanket," growled the lawman. He loosened his stance. "There *was* two of them. See how smooth that ground is? Someone spent some time here last night, or maybe after he could see this morning, dragging out the tracks under a blanket."

Doctor Nash faintly frowned. "Why?"

Instead of replying Whit strolled over the smoothed-out sandy soil until it faded out beside a clump of tall, spiked under-brush. "My guess is that the pouch might have been buried around here somewhere."

"Why would they hide it, if they thought they could get away scot-free?"

Whit shrugged. "Maybe because they weren't sure of that, Doc, and maybe because they didn't want to get caught with the money in their possession. Maybe a hundred things. Anyway, by now it's gone."

They scuffed around for a half hour before giving up as the heat steadily increased. The sun was still a long way off-centre but this time of year—summer—there did not have to be a yellow sun directly overhead to make the day hot.

"Now," said Whit as they walked back to the horses, "I've got to get the identity of that one in your shed, find out who he rode with, who was with him the last few weeks, then try to find that feller. Get out 'wanted' posters and letters—stuff like that."

They were untying when the peace officer also glumly said, "I've only corralled two men off 'wanted' dodgers in my life, Doc. That makes me wonder if other lawmen have ever done any better." He swung up. "If they haven't—there goes the darned army payroll, and along with it a piece of my reputation."

There was little Adrian Nash could say. He wanted to be cheerful, or at least reassuring, and on the ride back could not think of a single thing to say that would not sound downright dumb.

They had town in sight through shimmering layers of afternoon heat before Whit spoke again. "When the army comes I'll tell them it was probably some darned soldier or ex-soldier. Who else would know the exact stage to stop? And you know what they'll say? It was likely some coach-driver or gunguard, or maybe even Deacon Henderson, who knew and who set it up."

Doctor Nash sighed.

The town was retreating as it usually did this time of day. In fact it had already started to withdraw from heat and sunshine an hour or two earlier. There were only four horses at shaded tie-racks the full length of the roadway and they were out front of the stage office, draped with chain-harness awaiting the arrival of the north-bound stage up from along the border. All the rest of the tie-racks were empty and so was the roadway.

Down where the plankwalks ended, a yard or two north of the public trough and corrals which were north of the livery barn, a man was out front under a storefront overhang, sluicing water from a wooden bucket out into the roadway. This was supposed to hold down the heat. It didn't, but it did in fact settle the dust, except that today there were no horsemen to stir dust and no breeze either.

They parted out front and when Whit entered his cool old abode jailhouse, which had once been an *alcalde's* residence when the Southwest had belonged to Mexico, he flung his hat on a bench and went to the *olla* for water. Next to peppermint in the mouth when a man drank, the only really cold water in a desert town came from earthen jars called *ollas*. These seeped, so that evaporation kept the water inside them cool. They were commonly kept hanging so that air could reach completely around them. A person drank by tipping the thing. He was still tipping his *olla* when Deacon Henderson walked in, wiping perspiration off his square-jawed, ruddy face with a soiled shirt-cuff.

Before seating himself he said, "It wasn't no accident, Whit. The past couple months we've sent out two, sometimes three stages a day—and this one was the one he robbed. Now that don't fit the law of coincidence."

Marshal Whitsett went to his desk to drop down, damp and disgusted and a little tired. He had not got much sleep the preceding night; they had not got back to town with the dead outlaw until after midnight.

"What the hell is the law of coincidence?" he asked, unsmiling and gazing at the other man.

Deacon evaded that by saying, "Did you find the money-pouch?"

Whit had to shake his head.

Deacon's brows shot upward. "Didn't he have it on him?"

"All he had on him was two dollars' worth of silver, a shot-out Colt, some string in a little ball and a ragged old blue bandana along with a pocket-knife and some tobacco. No money-pouch."

"Well . . . what the hell did he do with it? I bet I know—he hid it. Cached it in them rocks up there."

"Doc and I just got back from looking

up there," stated the lawman and pulled
open a heavy drawer where he had been
placing 'wanted' dodgers for the past year
or so. Others he had in two cabbage crates
out in the back room. He pulled out a
handful of the posters. "You can help me
find out who he was, Deacon."

The stage company's local manager
stared at Marshal Turner Whitsett, not at
the stack of posters. "How in the hell . . . He
must have hid it right after the robbery."

"Possible," conceded Whit without
sounding convinced. He began reading
posters and putting them aside in another
stack. He was not going to admit to anyone
until he absolutely had to that he had been
outwitted; that there had been *two* of them
up there.

Deacon Henderson arose. "When folks
hear about this they're going to spade up
every darned foot of that country. If
someone finds that money, they sure as hell
won't hand it in."

Whit raised his eyes. "You're making it sound like it's my fault."

"Well, gawd-dammit, if you just set there looking at old outlaw posters when you'd ought to be up there diggin', it darned well might get to be your fault if someone else finds it, Whit."

The lawman's face faintly reddened. He did not remove his gaze as he said, "You got a spade, Deacon, and a wagon and some hired hands. You go dig it up." But as the other man turned toward the door, also red in the face, Turner Whitsett relented. "It's not up there. Doc and I made a pretty fair hunt."

Henderson's expression slowly changed; there was less indignation now and more puzzlement. "Then where is it?"

"I don't know."

Deacon waited, but when nothing more was volunteered he started to turn disagreeable again. "That's a hell of an answer. I sent in my report to Deming this

morning. They'll notify the army at Fort
Hannibal. Then what?"

"Then I expect the army will come over
here and rattle a few cages. Deacon, if I
could reach into the air and get your
money-pouch for you, I'd do it this minute,
otherwise, I got to do this like I'd do any
other kind of investigation, and that takes
time. I know—while someone maybe gets
hold of the army's money. Well, *I* didn't rob
the stage and I didn't put that darned
money aboard it."

Henderson stamped out into the
dancing heat-waves, ignoring them on his
way up the walk to his office, his truculent
face showing powerful anger.

Turner Whitsett did not feel anger, just
disgust and chagrin and a measure of per-
sonal shame. Last night he had not anticipated anything but this afternoon it seemed
to him that he should have. He'd run down
his share of stage-robbers; knew for a fact
they usually operated as teams. But last

night, in the dark, with that dead one lying there . . . "Hell," he growled and resumed looking through the stack of dodgers.

The worst part of it, although only he and Doctor Nash knew it, was that the second outlaw was in the saddle somewhere, putting a lot of miles between himself and the Buckeye area, and probably, by the time the law could even get close, he would have spent that money. That, as far as the army and a lot of other folks were concerned, was what would matter. Explaining how the law had to plod along in its pursuit never got a favourable reaction and for some reason people like Deacon Henderson and his employers, the ones responsible for that damned money being aboard the late-day south-bound stage, were the least understanding or patient.

He went through the stack of dodgers, separated four from the others, then went back over the four and discarded two of them. One of the discards was of a man who had been killed in Juarez; Whit remembered reading about that. The man had been killed last year so that eliminated him as a suspect. The remaining poster had the corpse's description in colouring and even his predilection for robbing stages fully spelled out. The name was Carl Brandon and he was one of those raffish Missourians whose dishonesty and worthlessness had been underscored by the James and Dalton brothers.

Whit wrote three letters for more information about Carl Brandon, then closed up the jailhouse, crossed to the saloon for his nightcap, gave Will Austen dour look for dour look and a half hour later went to the rooming-house to turn in—to lie awake in the sultry night turning things over and over in mind.

Hell, even if the dead one was Carl Brandon, that would confirm only one identification and not the important one at that.

From Brandon he would have to try and find out who Brandon had been riding with recently. *That* would be where the investigation would begin. Meanwhile that other one would be slathering greenbacks in the dancehalls and card-rooms and bars from Albuquerque to Denver.

He rolled up onto his side and within moments was asleep. Worry might interfere with sleep but not when a man was already dog-tired to begin with.

3

A SORREL HORSE

Reb Hunter who ran the livery barn met
Turner Whitsett at the café counter a half
hour ahead of sun-up, eased down with the
care of a man old enough to have brittle
bones and said, " 'Morning. Not a cloud in
the sky. Goin' to be a hell-scorcher today."
He flicked a dead fly off the oilcloth and
looked over to see what the marshal was
eating. "Them eggs fresh?" he asked, and
did not allow time for an answer. "Did you
talk to that lad I sent over half hour ago?"

Whit raised his head. "What lad?"

"Some lad about twelve, thirteen year' old. He was ridin' a big sorrel horse he'd found—saddled and bridled and all."

"Found?"

"Yep. Grazin' along draggin' his reins. He's got a tender back, I can tell you that without even runnin' a hand under the saddleblanket. I sent him up the back-alley to the jailhouse to hunt you up."

A sudden hope surged through Turner Whitsett. It was of course an impossibility, what he was suddenly contemplating, but he arose, tossed down some silver, nodded at the old liveryman and walked briskly across the road, down through and out back.

There was no lad back there but a big sorrel horse with hair dried flat from old sweat was standing patiently where he had been tied. Whit had no idea what colour horse that dead outlaw had been riding because there had been no horse around after the gunfight in the rocks. He had assumed the second outlaw had led it away with him.

A piping voice from the direction of the dog-trot to the north of Whit's jailhouse was followed by a gangling youth with a head of wildly unruly blond hair, freckles and a pair of steady grey eyes.

"Found him at our back corral in the evenin' last night, Mister Whitsett," the boy said, walking forward to stop beside the sorrel horse. "Just like that: saddled and bridled. My folks said I'd best fetch him down here to the law this morning. It's a fair ride, Mister Whitsett."

The boy seemed vaguely familiar but Whit had no idea who he was so he asked. The answer kept Whit standing there in total interest.

"I'm Ulysses Thorpe. My folks got a claim up along the foothills. We even got a spring of water on our homestead. We been puttin' together a herd of milk goats. Folks down here told my paw one thing Buckeye needs is milk, so we been puttin' together—"

"Whereabout, up along the foothills?" asked Whit.

"West of Gregorio Pass five, six miles where those old adobe buildings been for so long. Folks told us an old Messican had a ranch there one time and the In'ians wiped him out."

Whit knew now. That place had indeed been owned at one time by a Mexican, long before Whit's time but he'd been told the story by people over in Mex-town many times. How the Apaches had slipped down through the rocks, massacred the Mexican and ran off all his horses.

It was closer to six or seven miles from the mouth of Gregorio Pass. Whit turned without a word and studied the sorrel gelding. He had indeed been wearing that saddle and bridle a long time. He was a big strong animal, about six or seven years old, with a good, gentle intelligent eye and a pair of powerful front legs. The outfit showed wear but it too was well put-together and durable.

The boy said, "We figured some cowboy maybe forgot to tie his horse, or maybe the sorrel shied out from under someone."

Whit took down the tie-rope, removed the bridle, tied the horse with the shank and draped the bridle from the saddlehorn, then loosened the rear cinch first and finally tugged down the latigo to the front cinch. He dumped the rig in the dust. Sure enough, when he lay light fingers upon the sorrel horse's back the horse winced.

Ulysses said, "He's sure tender, ain't he?"

Whit tugged loose the shank. "Walk him down to the livery barn. Tell them to wash him good, all over, but mostly on the back, then stall him in the shade so's his back won't blister, then you come on back up the jailhouse and we'll talk."

The youth trudged southward without another word and Whit hoisted the outfit and entered through his back room into the jailhouse, hoping very hard there would be something here which would identify that corpse down in Doc's shed, because unless he was very mistaken this was the horse and outfit that dead outlaw had been riding.

It of course, as the boy had suggested, could belong to some rangerider. That idea had to be grudgingly faced. The one reason to suspect otherwise was that rangemen did not just forget a horse they had lost for a couple of days, especially in the area where they rode for someone. They hunted him down. No rider abandoned a lost horse, particularly if he was still wearing the rangeman's riding outfit.

The bridle was fairly typical. The headstall and reins were flat-plaited rawhide, common to the Southwest, and the bit was silver overlaid, also common to the Southwest. The saddle was old but made with the

deliberate thoughtfulness of men who created these outfits and who had usually been
riders themselves and understood how little
care the rig would get. The saddle-pockets
were part of the rear skirt, which, while
adding weight, also provided a rider with a
ready repository, which the old army-type
pockets, larger and made separately, did not
offer.

The saddlemaker's name had been
stamped into the seating-leather just
behind the gullet-opening. Many years of
trouser-cloth rubbing over it had obliter-
ated all but two words—"Wagonmound
New. . . ."

Wagonmound, New Mexico. Whit deci-
phered that with little difficulty but when
he tried to raise the maker's name he completely failed. Well hell, he told himself, it
wouldn't matter anyway, the saddle had
been made at least ten years earlier, maybe
even fifteen years earlier; the chances of the
maker still being over at the town of Wagon-

mound—or even alive for that matter—
were slim. Even slimmer was the possibility
of his remembering this particular outfit.
But most probable of all—the outlaw had
not bought this outfit new; rangemen rarely
did that for a very simple reason: they never
had that much money at one time.

He opened the left saddle-pocket.
There was a half-empty pony of malt
whisky in it. No label, just the bottle and
the amber liquid. He set the bottle atop the
desk and rolled the saddle to open the other
pocket.

There was a soiled leather-reinforced
coarse canvas pouch jammed inside with
the initials U.S.P.C. visible under ingrained
dust and dirt.

Whit's breathing stopped for two seconds. U.S.P.C. stood for United States Paymaster Corps. He slowly tugged out the
sack, slowly hefted it, found it heavy and
leaned to place it gently atop the desk.
Without looking at the saddle again he

went to a chair at the desk and sat down.

That second outlaw *hadn't* got it, then!

He rolled and lit a cigarette before freeing the top lacings to tip the sack and pour out the currency inside, then forgot the cigarette as he counted. The smoke was still dead between his lips when he began carefully stacking the greenbacks inside the sack. He did not relight the cigarette until he had locked the sack into a bottom desk drawer, was in fact lighting up when the lad walked in from out front.

Whit smiled and waved him to a chair, blew smoke and said, "When you found that horse last night, Ulysses, what did you do with him?"

"My paw said some rider'd be along directly for him and for me not to take off his outfit, just put him in the barn and fork some hay to him. Which is what I done, Mister Whitsett. Then, this morning right early when I went out with my paw to milk and feed the goats and all he said for me to

ride the horse down here and get shed of
him. Paw didn't like the idea. . . . He said
maybe someone would see us with him and
figure, us being homesteaders and all, that
we'd stole him. So I come down here
lookin' for you."

"No one showed up last night for him,
and you folks didn't look him over?"

"It was dark, Mister Whitsett," replied
the gangling youth, as though no one went
outside after nightfall, and Whit nodded,
crushed out his smoke and said, "How do
you figure to get back home?"

Ulysses answered easily. "Walk. I can
make it afore suppertime."

Whit stood up. "No, I got an extra horse
at the livery barn. You ride him back and in
a day or two I'll ride up and get him."

The boy's face lighted up.

Whit took Ulysses down to the livery
barn, sent the dayman for the horse and
until he had seen the lad on his way up the
back alley northward out of town he did

not look up the big sorrel horse. The dayman followed him to the stall with a wagging head. "Sure a pity the way some folks treat animals," he grumbled. "And that's a right nice horse. Stout as a mule and sound as new money. He's worth a little money. You got any idea who might have lost him?"

Whit watched the freshly washed horse stand at the manger to eat while he completely ignored the pair of men at the stall door and did not answer except to say, "Must be worth maybe fifty dollars."

The dayman agreed with that. "All of fifty dollars. You'd think folks would take better care if for no better reason than because he's worth that much, wouldn't you?"

Whit nodded and turned. "Tell your boss he's impounded by the law," he said and strolled back to the bright sunlight leaving the dayman looking after him. He had impounded horses before, but only when someone had broken the law and as far as the dayman knew, losing your horse wasn't against the law. Not even neglecting him the way this horse had been neglected, although it had always seemed to the dayman there should have been a law against abuse.

Whit returned to the office, hauled the dead outlaw's bridle and saddle and blanket to the back room and left them there, then went back to rattle the lower desk-drawer to reassure himself it was still locked, and tossed aside his hat beginning to feel enormously relieved finally. He was not a man who whooped for joy nor turned instantly ecstatic over good fortune.

It was easily ten degrees cooler inside his thick-walled jailhouse than it was out in the roadway, even this early in the morning. He stoked the stove, put his old coffeepot atop it, then turned with his back to the heat and was lost in thought when Adrian Nash walked in looking dusty and unshaven. He smiled, put his little satchel and his hat upon the bench next to the door and sniffed at the rising aroma of coffee.

"People never have babies except in the middle of the night," Nash said, not complaining particularly, just making a statement of fact in a tone of resignation. "Is that coffee ready?"

"In a few minutes," replied the lawman, strolled to the desk, unlocked the drawer and set the soiled paymaster's pouch in plain view on the desk.

Doctor Nash stared. "Where in hell did you find it?"

Whit explained about the homesteader's kid and the sorrel horse. Doc sat down and studied the pouch for a moment. "Empty?"

"Full, Doc. There's eleven hundred dollars in it, not nine hundred like Deacon thought."

Doc let his breath out slowly, still gazing at the pouch. "Put the damned thing out of sight, Whit," he eventually said, and Whit dropped the sack back into its drawer, turned the key and went over to see if the coffee was ready. It was. He filled two cups and took one over to Doc with a thin smile.

"The question now is, Doc—will he come back and try to find it? Is he maybe up there in the hills right now tryin' to pick up the tracks of his partner's horse? I'll tell you one thing he is sure as hell doing— kicking himself for not putting the pouch into his own saddlebags."

Doc sipped coffee before speaking. "Can he find the tracks?"

"Yeah. But he's got to do it in daylight. What I been standin' here wondering is— did he try to find them yesterday?"

"And?"

"The answer is no—because if he had he'd have tracked the sorrel to the squatter's barn and there wouldn't be any pouch in my drawer right now."

Doc pondered this before slowly nodding his head as he finished the coffee and gazed over the rim of the cup at Turner Whitsett. "Which means . . . today, maybe?"

"I figure it like that. *If* he's up there and if he's going to try and find the pouch at all."

"He'll try, Whit. I would and so would you, after going through all that and being this close to getting it. He'll try."

Doc slapped his legs and arose. "Let me change and shave and I'll meet you at the barn. An hour—no—half an hour."

"You just got back from delivering a baby. You been up most of the night, Doc."

Nash was at the door, little satchel in hand, hat on the back of his head when he said, "Doctors don't need sleep. Ask anyone, they'll tell you that." He smiled and went out into the pleasant early morning brilliance.

Whit had another cup of coffee, speculated about putting the money-pouch in the iron safe up at the general store, decided not to just yet because he would prefer not to have word spread over town that the pouch had been recovered and took a booted Winchester from a corner behind the desk, re-set his hat and went out, locking the jailhouse door from outside before strolling southward to the livery barn.

If people saw him like that, booted carbine slung over his shoulder, it could not be helped. *That* much the town could speculate about.

The dayman too, when he saw Whit walk in, looked twice. The only time Turner Whitsett rode with a saddlegun was when he went hunting in the autumn—and this was early summer—or when he was riding out for some serious purpose. The dayman went at once to get a horse.

Outside, morning was brightening the entire desert countryside with a cool, soft, golden glow. It was the best time of day on the south desert. The faraway northward low hills looked five miles closer than they actually were and every unkempt little fat juniper tree upon their rolling low heights was clearly visible.

4

A WAIT

To ride due northward up the stageroad would make their presence known—if there was anyone up there watching and he was riding with that thought in mind—so Turner Whitsett turned off westward and did not alter course again for almost two miles. They were on the northward leg of their trip before they saw movement. It was a band of wild cattle; they took one look at the pair of oncoming horsemen and fled.

Doctor Nash watched their swift progress after making a tart observation. "Anyone who would *want* to handle animals like that deserves the broken bones I set every riding season."

Whit was looking for the homesteaders' buildings and said nothing until he finally made them out and pointed. "That's where the sorrel horse was last night—with the saddlepockets on him." He looked along the westerly rocky foothills, not really expecting to see someone over there, nor did he see anyone. No movement at all, in fact, not even more cattle or horses.

They did not approach the adobe buildings of the Thorpe place, but went far out and around to reach the brakes beyond, northwesterly. Then they turned back slowly, keeping to cover even when it took them momentarily out of their way.

Adrian Nash never once questioned what Turner Whitsett was doing. It was still a beautiful morning; anyone cooped up in town most of the week would have been as relaxed and comfortable as Doc Nash was.

They halted, finally, where a seepage spring made an oasis of about three acres. There were even several cottonwood trees in this place, a rarity anywhere on the south desert unless there was abundant water.

Doc piled off, skived mosquito larvae off a clearwater pool, drank, then allowed his horse to do the same as he got back upright, thumbed back his hat and looked all around. "It's something you have to like from the soul, Whit, this desert country, or you can't stand it."

Whit was watering his horse before tying it to a bush. He had no comment to offer concerning the desert. If he hadn't liked it he would not have put in the last seven years on it.

They went south a quarter mile to a fat, low lift of gritty land and got atop it where stirrup-high bunch grass grew, pale almost as straw and with seed-heads just now beginning to cure. In the old days the

Indians had brought a blanket with them. One would hold the blanket like a trough while another one would strike the tall heads with a flat stick, knocking grass seed into the blanket. It was a primitive way to harvest edible seed but it had kept Indians alive and flourishing for centuries—maybe even for millenia.

They lay flat in the grass, their scope of visibility adequate. They could see the squatter's set of old buildings on their right, miles of broken foothills marked here and there by boulder-fields on their left. Southward they could just barely make out Buckeye's rooftops. Once, when a morning stage went flogging it southward down from Gregorio Pass, they saw the dust strung out like a diaphanous, tawny banner, the coach out front dwarfed to toy size by intervening distance.

Doc yawned and tipped down his hat to minimise reflection off the pale grass. "He'd better come soon or I'm going to fall asleep," he said.

Whit had no objection. "Go ahead. If I see anything I'll elbow you awake."

Doc did in fact fall asleep with the warm sun on his back and shoulders, with the vast depth of desert silence on all sides, with that uniquely deceptive benignity of the south desert working its specific spell.

Whit had never been an individual who abandoned an idea easily and fortunately he had the patience for this kind of disposition. The sun climbed, heat came, nothing moved anywhere and he did not give up, did not even think the second outlaw—the one who could kill his own partner with a bullet in the back of the head—would not appear.

He saw someone herding small animals over in the direction of the homesteader's claim, assumed it was either Ulysses or his father taking their milk-nannies out to browse and a little later he saw three rangeriders pass eastward in the direction

of the stageroad, from off to the west somewhere, riding loosely and casually as most
cowmen rode. But that was all and the sun
continued to climb.

Doc awakened thirsty, raised himself up
to look around then said, "What's holding
him back?"

"Maybe he's smart, Doc. Maybe he figures to wait until it's so hot folks won't be
abroad."

"Is that so? Well, maybe he'll be right."
Doc squinted at the overhead pale yellow
disc. "You could fry eggs atop the rocks. I'd
trade a silver dollar for a drink from an old
rusty canteen right about now."

Whit did not smile when he said, "If
you don't sweat you won't need water,
Doc."

The physician looked over. "It's a hundred and ten degrees at least. How do you
not sweat?"

Whit did not reply. He was watching
distant movement off on their left. It could

be a rider. It could also be someone's horse walking along or maybe a calvy cow which had quit a bunch to go into the seclusion of the brakes to calve. He did not comment until the movement worked its way back and forth among the low upthrusts, in and out and around boulder-fields and through a stand of stunted timber to emerge finally only a mile and a half distant, then he pointed.

"Horseman."

Doc forgot his thirst and the heat to twist and stare.

For a while the rider did not reappear and that worried Doc. He did not admit this but kept fidgeting until the horseman walked his mount around the low, fat shoulder of a landswell, coming into full sight again. Doc dropped a little lower, but the rider could not see them; as long as they did not stand up he would have no reason to suspect they were atop their knoll. Whit was silent for ten minutes, until he had made up his mind, then he resignedly said, "He's not following tracks. Watch him, he never once looks at the ground, he just pokes along."

"It's got to be him," exclaimed Doctor Nash.

The rider got fairly close as he swerved to pass around the base of their knoll. He was riding a hip-shot old mare, grey as a badger and lean in the flank. The man was wearing flat-heeled boots of the variety used by squatters—and freighters and even some townsmen—but not stockmen. He had an old Colt around his middle but no carbine, no saddlebags, and never once looked behind nor even to his left nor right except now and then, the way a bored rider might do.

Whit said, "Homesteader," and Doctor Nash swore a little in disgust.

After the rider had passed along, evidently heading for the Thorpe place, Whit looked at the sun. It was off-centre by several degrees and it was pouring molten heat downward in shimmering layers. Whit said, "Not today, Doc. I was pretty sure he'd do it, but I guessed wrong."

Doc was baffled. "He surely wouldn't just give up."

"He might. He might figure we found the money-pouch and decide it was too hot for him down here. I'm like you—I didn't figure he'd give up this easy, though."

Doc was dogged about this. "Nor would he. For some darned reason he's not reacting as he should, but you can bet your horse and saddle he wouldn't just up and ride off. Not knowing that money-sack was still down here somewhere. I don't believe it, Whit."

Whether Doc was right or wrong one thing was certain—the outlaw was not in sight, which meant he was not coming. If he'd been back-tracking that sorrel horse he would have certainly shown up before this.

Whit lifted his hat, mopped sweat, re-settled the hat and twisted around to scan the rearward hills, but there was nothing to be seen up there, no movement even. He settled forward wishing the knoll-top had a few trees on it like some knolls had. Not that this would have mitigated the heat but it certainly would have diluted direct sunlight. He finally shook his head. "Let's go, Doc."

They went back to the horses, cinched up and rode southward out into the open country where sunlight had a good shot at them. A mile out they tipped down their hats and Doc's thirst increased until he no longer much cared to make light of it.

There was no water between the foothills and town but no one could die in that distance although, as Doctor Nash could certify by the time they got back to Buckeye in the early evening, a person could become very uncomfortable.

He went over to the saloon for a glass of beer first, then went back to his cottage for a follow-up of water. In fact he continued to drink water until suppertime before his system no longer required it. Then he ambled down to the café, half-expecting to encounter Whit there but the caféman said Whitsett had not been in since breakfast time. Later Doc went over to the jailhouse with pearly dusk beginning benignly to settle. The jailhouse was locked from the outside, there was no light in the office and Doctor Nash stood frowning for a moment before turning southward to walk as far as the livery barn.

The nighthawk was on duty. All he could say was that Marshall Whitsett had taken a fresh horse and the sorrel and had gone up the alley with them an hour earlier. Doctor Nash asked several questions, got shrugs or head-shakes, gave it up and returned to the quiet, dusky roadway to ponder.

Finally he went out back of the jail-house, but there was no sign of a horse there, let alone two horses, so he went up to his place to filch some stogies from a box in the kitchen, fill a canteen at the sink-pump, lock up and with the canteen slung from his shoulder return down the back-alley to the livery barn.

He only owned one horse, a combination buggy-saddle beast, and he did not want to make it go out again so he had to hire a horse, which annoyed him even though he knew he would never have to pay out any cash; old Reb Hunter was forever haunting Doc's anteroom with some kind of ache or pain or complaint. Doc would deduct this horse he was now straddling from the next office visit.

He had an idea where Whit had gone. He also had evolved an idea about why Whit had gone up there and what he was going to do.

He did not feel exactly delighted at the prospect of riding out again so soon. Not that he did not like horsebacking, it was just that his rear and his legs were not accustomed to this much of it. Tomorrow he would pay with stiffness.

But the night for all its enduring heat was pleasant and before too long it might turn slightly cooler. At any rate there was no dehydrating sunlight. But if there had been Doc was prepared this time. That canteen slogged along from its strap around the saddlehorn.

If he'd been compelled to explain why he was doing this he could not have given a very satisfactory reply, except that he was curious and he had been involved from the beginning—still had that corpse out back in his shed; a man couldn't get much more involved than that—and there was another reason: he liked Turner Whitsett. Maybe Doctor Nash was a little like disagreeable Deacon Henderson; when he had faith in someone it bothered him to believe they might fail, made him feel that he too had a stake in their success. But whatever it was,

Doc was half way to the foothills before the moon arrived over a tree-fringed far hillock and by then the night was finally beginning to turn slightly cooler. Not very much cooler—Doc was still perspiring under his shirt and coat—but a little cooler, with a promise of additional coolness to come.

5

ANOTHER RIDE

Whit approached the squatter's place from the southwest in about the same direction he and Doctor Nash had used that morning. He halted a mile out, when he was able to discern wavery orange candle-glow on his right, left the pair of saddled horses in a copse of spindly pines and went ahead on foot.

He had all night, or felt he probably had at least half or two-thirds of it, and for what he had in mind he might even have all the rest of his life, because his shrewdness today had not paid off, so there was no reason to believe this scheme would either, in which case he'd have to learn to live with failure.

But he had to try it. He'd perfected it during the last long silence when he and Doc had been approaching town just ahead of early evening. It was, he felt, his last throw of the dice. If this scheme also failed, he was back where he had started from—except that he had the payroll money—and that made a lot of difference. He no longer felt the pressures. Now, he was manhunting because he wanted a murderer. Maybe neither Deacon Henderson nor Will Austen, nor other folks, would believe that was important once they understood the money-pouch had been recovered, but *Whit* felt it was important.

Also, failure earlier had made him a little more dogged. The argument his friends would have used—that as long as renegades killed each other decent folk benefited—had been tried on him a lot of times. His answer had always been the same. They *didn't* always kill each other; they didn't in fact kill one another very much at all, they killed decent folks.

He stood motionless a hundred yards from the squatter's thick-walled old adobe buildings looking, listening, sensing how it was up here and finally, satisfied there was no dog, or if there were, he was probably inside because he had not come out to challenge Whit noisily, he moved on around—out of shotgun range—to the made-over animal shelter which now served as a barn. Mexicans rarely put doors on sheds. They had two very excellent reasons for not doing this. One was that in a country where the wind rarely blew and where it seldom rained, they did not need doors. The other reason was that planed timber suitable for making doors was prohibitively expensive. It had to reach the south desert by freight wagon. There were no merchantable trees down there and what timber there was, such as cottonwood—and not much of that—was not even fit for cook-stoves.

But there was a door on the squatter's barn. Not of planed lumber though. It had been created of faggots wired very closely together the way Mexicans made many of their corrals. The idea was not that these things were strong; they were not; in fact a stout billy-goat could butt his way through. But they could not be seen through and that would stop even the wildest horse.

Inside, the adobe building with its three-foot-thick walls and its windowless-ness had an intensity of darkness not even a moonless night could match. It smelled of goats. They had an open passageway from this adobe barn to a faggot corral out back. Evidently they were all out there because Whit heard little rustling sounds and now and then a high, short bleat.

He took his time exploring the place,

found two tie-stalls side by side, felt a manger, felt a tie-ring, turned and familiarised himself with the little building, then went back outside and started back.

Someone inside was probably reading or perhaps sewing or mending or maybe even setting out breaddough to rise because there was still candle-light as Whit headed back for the sorrel horse.

The two animals nickered, not very loudly, and he thought they might have detected his return but when he got closer he heard another horse walking up-country with a measured stride.

He palmed a gun, trotted south of his horses to make the interception where if there were trouble it would not be close enough to stampede his two animals, then he squatted to skyline the oncoming rider, saw him, caught a good view of him and slowly began to shake his head. Then he stood up and holstered the Colt and waited.

"What in the hell," he said finally, "do you think you are doing, Doc?"

"Getting a little night air. It's very good for clogged sedimentary and respiratory—"

"How did you know I'd be up here?"

Doctor Nash dismounted, gazing up where the candle-light was discernible. "We didn't catch him by out-waiting him, so the next logical thing to do is to use bait to catch him." Doc smiled and looked at the big sorrel horse. "Well; if you wish I'll mind the house while you slip around back there and put the horse back in the barn. But Whit—no one is going to expect him to still be saddled and bridled, are they?"

Instead of answering the marshal grunted, turned and untied the sorrel, then walked off through the darkness with him.

Doc fingered a cigar, would have enjoyed its pungent companionship, returned it reluctantly and studied the squat adobe structures up ahead, north-ward from him.

The night was agreeably warm, stars were cast across a great dark vastness like shiny, large grains of sand and if there were a moon it had not arrived yet.

By the time Marshal Whitsett returned Doc had decided being a lawman demanded more of a man than he got paid to do. For example, tonight other respectable folk were decently abed and Turner Whitsett was out here putting the finishing touches upon a day which had been at least fifteen hours long—so far, and they weren't back to town yet.

Whit shoved back his hat, looked from Doc back toward the house and said, "The longer it goes like this the less I figure our chances are. If he don't come looking for the horse by morning, Doc—"

"We've lost him. Yes, I know. I've been speculating about that." Doc asked if Whit intended to spend the night up here and got an affirmative nod, so he decided he might as well do the same but wanted to stroll a short distance back southward so they could smoke.

Down there, saddles loosened, bridles draped and horses hobbled to browse if they cared to, Doctor Nash said, "And if he doesn't show up?"

Whit shrugged. He was not too upset over losing this outlaw. If he hadn't recovered the loot from Deacon Henderson's stage he would have been upset more. "Go through the usual routine, Doc—send out dodgers and maybe someday he'll show up and get grabbed. More'n likely what'll happen would be he'd be dyin' of old age and would want to clear his conscience." Whit smiled in the darkness. "Every time you read about lawmen catchin' one, figure that he's got five more in his files he don't catch."

"Bad percentage, Whit. If I figured my patients that way it would be demoralising."

"You lose 'em all, Doc. It just takes longer." Whit stubbed out his smoke and eyed the sky, then gazed northward. "I keep being less hopeful," he murmured.

Doctor Nash said nothing but he probably felt the same way. He gave a slight start when a thick-bodied big trotting wolf crossed above them between where they were hunkering and the homesteader's old buildings. The wolf had not picked up any scent, obviously, and since they had not been moving he had not had his attention attracted.

Abruptly one of the browsing horses snorted. That was all it took. The wolf sensed danger in one second and became a blur of phantom-grey.

Whit said, "The goats," then he also said, "He should have picked up tobacco-smoke scent a mile away. Probably an old cuss."

"Large," stated Doctor Nash. "I've never seen that large a wolf before."

Whit had seen them that large but never before on the desert. He had no explanation to offer for this and while he was listening to the diminishing sounds of the large predator another sound caught and held his attention. Someone up among the adobes northward had either bumped a pan against something or had deliberately struck it.

Whit waited for the sound to be repeated. It never was. Doc was not especially concerned. "Someone washing before retiring just flung the basinful of water out the back door."

It was reasonable. Whit remained motionless low along the ground gazing northward. "Why are they up so late?" he asked quietly. "It's past ten, Doc."

Nash offered no reply but he looked slowly from Whit to the buildings, toward the particular building where candlelight still faintly glowed.

There of course was a long list of possible reasons which could explain why someone up there had not retired. If it were the woman, because she had got behind with her work and was trying to catch up now with her mending or baking or maybe even soap-making. If it was her husband he might be hunching over a table trying with pencil and paper to devise a way to squeeze another few coppers from his milk-goats.

Doc yawned, looked elsewhere in the night, then looked back up there. "What's on your mind?" he asked.

Whit made a hard chuckle when he said, "Darned if I know. I was just wondering, is all."

Doc glanced northward again. "I know how we can find out why someone up there isn't in bed."

Whit arose. "Let's go."

He was not actually suspicious, he was simply curious, and if there had been anything else to occupy his attention he would not even have been curious.

They did not get very close. A man's clear voice came out to them as though he were standing close. He said, "It's not hard to figure out and you just better leave it plumb where it is."

Whit halted with Doc at his side. They waited a long while for an answer, but there was not one or if there was it must have been whispered because neither of the waiting men south of the house heard it.

There was no other sound either.

Whit finally beckoned and started far out and around with Doctor Nash following. They got up within sighting distance of the adobe shed where Whit had left the sorrel horse before halting. There was a distinct aroma of smoking up here. Whit stood a long while in thoughtful silence, then jerked his head for Doc to follow along and retreated a hundred yards.

Having had a lesson in how well sounds carried on this night Whit went far enough back to be safe before saying, "It's beginning to get a little complicated, Doc."

Nash smiled slightly in the darkness. "I would say it is. I would say instead of a simple matter of someone coming along looking for a horse, Whit, there is the man looking for the horse and another man warning him against taking the horse or saddlebags. He said it wasn't hard to figure out . . . They are guessing we are out here."

Whit turned back to look eastward where the buildings were vaguely noticable. "You ever talk to this settler, Doc?"

"Nope."

"Neither have I, so that could have been him talking or it could have been someone else . . . Doc?"

"Yes."

"If you were just riding back, say, from tending some sick squawman back in the mountains, and got thirsty or hungry or something as you came down here and saw the light. . . ."

Nash was scowling. "What for? Just so's I can afterwards tell you whether that voice belonged to this settler?"

"Partly. Partly to keep him inside while

I scour around out here." Doc was not
enthusiastic but eventually he walked down
where they had left the horses. Whit heard
him crossing to the north by circling wide
around the buildings out back. It was not a
settled conviction in Whit's mind that the
settler was in any way involved in something illegal. Even if an outlaw was using
the homestead as perhaps a hideout it was
not likely the homesteader would be very
involved. Not improbable, but not very
likely either.

Until he had heard that sentence
spoken into the clear night a few yards from
the main adobe he was perfectly willing to
believe the sorrel horse had strayed this far.
He still felt this was what had happened;
that the sorrel had been found as the lad
named Ulysses had said. And if there were
involvement, that settler never would have
sent the horse to town with his son and
with that intact money-pouch.

But—there was something up here he

was curious about and that one spoken sentence was the basis for his interest.

He went back to the adobe barn and got inside into darkness so complete that although he could smell the sorrel horse and even hear him moving a little now and then he could not see him. He knew where he had draped the saddle from a pole and felt his way to it. He had placed the rig in a particular way. It had been moved. The pockets were still buckled, but the rig had been pawed and shifted slightly.

He worked his way along until he was back near the rear opening, paused to listen for a long moment, then slipped outside.

The night beyond, even without much moonglow, seemed clear after the inside of that horse-shed. He picked a soundless way over in the direction of what he knew was a chicken-house because he had seen a few scrawny hens in the outside compound behind the little adobe shed.

Doc came noisily down between the

barn and house, allowing his horse to plod
on a loose rein as though they were both
tired. Doc halted and hailed the house from
his saddle. Whit blinked, when the door
opened, and faded out over alongside the
hen-house. He heard Doc tell his believable
lie, heard the homesteader invite Doc to get
down and come inside and watched as a
woman in a high-necked, very long, plain,
pale dress held the door for Doc while her
man went forth to lead Doc's horse away.

Whit prayed the homesteader would
not be a good enough horseman to discern
that Doc's horse had not been ridden
down.

Later, when the homesteader returned
across the yard in long strides, Whit turned
to open the hen-house door. It was locked.
In fact it was locked from the inside. Whit
ran his hands up and down the door on
both sides, top and bottom, and could find
no latch. He wondered how, if they locked
the hen-house from the inside, they after-

wards got outside, and moved down the far side of the old adobe building seeking another door. The run out back was made of slatted palings set very close together, so close a chicken could do no more than get its head between the faggots.

There was a gate. Whit opened it and stepped inside certain he would now encounter a rear-wall door. What he found was a small square opening in the lower middle of the thick mud wall where chickens came and went, but no passageway large enough to accomodate a man or a woman.

No one locked a hen-house from inside, then tried to crawl through a chicken exit that small in the rear wall. He examined the walls with rising interest until he was back around front again. The world suddenly exploded with a roaring sound which was accompanied by a blinding brilliance and a sensation of heat running all through his body.

6

"Your Friend Is A Murderer"

There was a pleasant coolness and a shading of pale light when Whit opened his eyes. He was lying upon a fresh sifting of straw in the chicken house with the dawn-light appearing through that small square hole in the lower back wall. He could smell chickens without being able to see any. When he moved, though, rustling the hay, chickens made low sounds so there was a perch of them in there somewhere.

His neck hurt more than his head. He had to lie a while trying to recall how he had gotten in here. When realisation eventually arrived he felt his holster. It was empty. He felt a rear pocket; the wallet was still there, so was the pocket-knife in his front pocket and his hat had been shoved beneath his head.

There should have been a lump but evidently his hat had protected him from direct contact with that gunbarrel or whatever it was he had been crowned with.

He lifted his head, the muscles of his neck reacted with pain so he eased back and for a while simply lay there. Except for being in a chicken house he was comfortable enough.

The smell of tobacco smoke lingered too, discernible among the other odours. He remembered Doc Nash, wondered about him and heard the chickens murmuring, moving a little, and looked for them. There was a graduated perch made of faggots along the east wall. They were up there acting as though they were about to get down. Chickens were early risers; if these were getting ready for the new day it had to be about dawn. He knew that without the chickens telling him from the increasing paleness of the grey light.

Outside a horse nickered and moments later a man's bootsteps grinding into yard-dust sounded louder as they approached the chicken house.

Whit reached with his right hand to support his head so that his neck would cause less pain and sat up with straw clinging to him.

The door opened, a man moved inside, saw Whit sitting there and stopped dead in his tracks, then he said, speaking swiftly, "I thought you was gone. Where's the old horse, then?"

Whit studied the man. He was tall and lanky, dressed in patched shirt and old faded work-trousers, had washed and combed his hair this morning but had not shaved. He did not wear a gunbelt and the smell which came in with him was not of horses but of goats.

Whit said, "Is your name Thorpe?"

The man did not move and he did not answer for a long time. "Yes . . . I made a mistake. I thought you was someone else."

Whit bunched himself to arise and afterwards as he beat off chaff he dryly said, "I guess you did for a fact figure I was someone else." He straightened around. "Where's your friend, the feller who's been staying in this chicken house?"

"Who?"

Whit did not argue nor raise his voice, he simply pointed to the latch on the inside of the door. "You got awful smart chickens, Mister Thorpe; they lock themselves in at night. And they got a nice straw bed to sleep on—man-size." He watched the homesteader's face begin to show fear, then he said, "I'm Turner Whitsett, marshal down at Buckeye. I'll ask you once more— where is that son of a bitch who was inside here last night, who hit me over the head— the scrawny-looking individual riding that bony old snake of a settler-horse who rode over here to see you yesterday?"

Thorpe shot a look back outside as though to either run or make sure no one could hear them, then he swung back. "I don't know," he said.

"But you told him last night not to take the horse and outfit, that it wasn't hard to figure out—that horse and saddle being back in your shed."

Thorpe studied Whit with a doleful expression on his face. "I just know this feller rode in and asked if we'd seen a sorrel horse with a saddle an' bridle on him. I told him we'd found the horse and my boy had taken him on down to Buckeye to turn him over to the law. That's all, Marshal."

Whit raised a hand to lightly massage

his sore neck, then bent to retrieve his hat, beat straw off it and punch it back into shape. He did all this without looking again at the homesteader or speaking to him. But after he had gently put the hat on he said, "Mister Thorpe, you're not too good at lying."

"He rode in here and said—"

"You already told me that."

"It's the truth. If I'd had anything to do with him why would I have sent my son down yonder with that horse and the money-pouch?"

"That's what I'm trying to figure out, Mister Thorpe, and the lad told me no one had looked in the saddlebags, so how did you know it was a money-pouch?"

"Well; I looked, but I didn't take the pouch out and I didn't want my boy to know, so I never told him I'd looked; just told him to make a bee-line and deliver the outfit to you. Marshal, if I'd been partners with that feller, you think I'd have sent the

horse and pouch down to you? Not likely;
I'd have at least got part of the money. Lord
knows we could use it; could use any
amount of money at all."

"Mister Thorpe, that feller arrived at
your place kind of early yesterday and he
was still here in the hen-house late last
night and he'd been here before, had slept
here and had fixed that latch to work from
the inside."

They gazed at each other a long time
before Whit also said, "Where's Doctor
Nash?"

Thorpe slumped and turned to watch
his hens climbing down from the
wall-perch to go outside to start their daily
scratching.

"The doctor's over at the house eating
breakfast. He never mentioned you, nor
riding out here with anyone else. He said
he'd been up in the mountains lookin' after
some old sourdough trapper who—"

"Let's go over to the house, Mister

Thorpe."

The settler's body pulled up straight. "No. Marshal, my wife's not a well person."

"Well, Mister Thorpe, I don't feel too good right now myself."

"Please, Marshal. . . ."

Whit read the lined, long weathered face of the other man correctly. "Your wife didn't know about this feller camping in your hen-house?"

". . . No."

That was the first admission and Whit moved to take quick advantage of it. "I'm going to take you to town, and lock you up. Then I'm going to ferret out this whole darned mess and I particularly want to meet that feller who hit me over the head last night."

Thorpe's anxiety deepened, but he began to also look a little sick as he said, "I'll tell you the whole story, only let me go over first and get my wife and boy out of the house."

"How?"

"She was going berry-picking this morning, before it gets hot. Her and Ulysses. Let me go over and get them clear away first, Marshal."

"There's a good stout sorrel horse in the shed, Mister Thorpe."

"I give you my word. You can watch the shed from here and if I go over there—"

"I'll shoot a leg out from under you," replied Whit, forgetting he no longer had a gun.

Thorpe seemed to sense that he was going to be allowed to leave. He said, "You got my word, Marshal. Just let me get them away first."

Whit nodded. "Tell Doc where I am. Tell him to wait in the house. Mister Thorpe . . ." Their eyes met and there was no doubt about the steeliness in the lawman's gaze.

Thorpe backed out of the hen-house and went shuffling across the yard. Whit

watched him from around the ajar door—
then felt the empty holster. He swore, but
did nothing. One thing he had learned long
ago was that strong family men did not
abandon their wives and children. He
intended to use this as his lever in getting
everything out of this settler that the man
knew. He had used this, in fact, as the basis
for his present strategy of allowing the
homesteader to send his wife and son away.
The man would be too shattered in spirit to
say anything in front of his wife and son
once they knew he had been involved with
an outlaw.

Maybe it was not customary lawman
procedure, but then Turner Whitsett had
never conformed to much that was supposed to govern the action of lawmen.

He massaged his neck again. It hurt
much more than his head did. In fact, he
had awakened many a morning in his life-
time with this same small kind of dull
headache just from having one shot of

green whiskey and it had usually passed by mid-morning. He had a thick skull. He had also discovered that a long while ago.

Five nanny-goats with undulating udders walked forth, golden-coloured pop eyes brightly alert as they headed across the yard southward, out where there was browse. Whit briefly watched, remembered that old wolf last night, thought he had probably been attracted by the powerful scent of the goats and also speculated that if Whit and Doc had not been out there to frighten that wolf, he probably would have gotten himself a meal of milk-goat in the wee hours.

The woman came out wearing a bonnet and carrying two old baskets, one of which she turned to hand to her son. Whit remembered the lanky lad. This morning his trousers and shirt were just as threadbare, and he was barefoot, but he looked clean, as did his attire.

Whit studied the woman. She was tall

and lithe. He could not make out her face beneath the jutting curve of her bonnet, but she had dark hair, he could see that, and she did not act very old, perhaps thirty-five. She was a well-built woman. Whit spat cotton. For some reason he was very thirsty, as he watched the lad and his mother hike around between the house and horse-shed. He watched intently but neither of them even glanced in that direction. They seemed to be hurrying, perhaps so that they could get to the berry-patch, wherever it was—probably a fair distance or they wouldn't be hurrying—and back before the full force of the desert sun arrived.

Whit rolled a smoke, lit it, moved his head left and right, found that none of the neck-ache had departed and looked behind him where two hens were standing near a boxnest looking up at him.

He said, "Well, go ahead and climb in and lay your darned eggs, I'm not going to bother you."

But they must have thought otherwise because they both ducked out that square little low hole and disappeared into the yard.

As he faced forward again he saw Doc and the homesteader approaching, so evidently Thorpe had told Doc about Whit. There was another scrap of information Whit was shortly to learn: That outlaw had left his old bony nag and had taken the stout sorrel horse.

Whit and Doc exchanged a look, then Whit glanced sourly at the homesteader. "You didn't mention that before," he said, knowing perfectly well why it had not been mentioned; because up until this moment the settler had not been entirely willing to make disclosures.

Doc examined the slight lump under Whit's hat, felt his neck, worked it around, then said, "You're all right."

Whit did not smile. "I could have told

you that."

"But you wouldn't be if you didn't have a skull of granite." Doc was smiling. "There are some flapjacks and syrup left at the house."

They walked slowly across the yard in the pleasant early sunlight as Whit said, "Did your friend say where he got those old clothes and that old horse he was riding?"

Thorpe seemed uncomfortable as he replied. "Said he stole them from a home-steader three, four miles on the east side of the stageroad."

"He figured someone might be watching for him?"

"Yes. But they wouldn't pay no mind to one settler riding over to visit another set-tler."

"Did he tell you how that sorrel horse happened to have that money-pouch on him?"

"Yes; he said the horse run away from him right after he robbed a stagecoach over near that pass through the hills."

Doc and Whit exchanged a glance before the lawman spoke again. "Did he tell you he had a partner in that robbery?"

"No. He just said—"

"He had one, Mister Thorpe—and he shot him in the back of the head."

Thorpe stopped stone-still near the open door of the house. "Killed him . . . ?"

"Deader'n a rock, Mister Thorpe. Your friend is a murderer. You helpin' him makes you an accessory to murder."

Thorpe turned like a man in a trance and entered with the other two men following after, watching him. He went to the old iron stove and flipped warm pancakes onto a tin dish and brought it to the oil-cloth-covered, rickety table without raising his eyes.

Whit sat down with a sigh. "Water," he said, and Thorpe brought him a tin cup full. After Whit had downed it he held forth the cup for a refill and as the homesteader returned to the bucket in a shady corner Whit said, "You want to help? Just start right at the beginning, Mister Thorpe."

Nothing more was said for a while until Thorpe had put the refilled tin cup atop the table and was watching Whit eat. The silence might have gone farther but Doctor Nash broke it by saying, "I'm curious about something, Mister Thorpe. How did you happen to get into the goat-milk business?"

Thorpe's dull gaze lifted to Doc's face with a look of disbelief. "The goat-milk business? That's not important right now."

Doc did not yield. "It is to me. Why, Mister Thorpe?"

"Because my wife's not a well person. She gets them awful stomach pains. Sometimes she can't hardly get up from bed in the morning and one time a friend, another settler from west a couple miles, fetched over a bucket of goat milk. My wife drank it; she felt better right away."

"So you got some milk-goats too."

Thorpe nodded. "Yes sir. Then I worked up a little trade deliverin' it around Buckeye. That's our only source of cash money."

Doctor Nash considered his hands as he quietly said, "Why didn't you bring your wife to me in town if you knew she was that sick?"

Thorpe flung his arms wide. "And pay you with what, Doctor? I don't have a dime."

Doc continued to gaze at his hands. "You wouldn't have to pay me." He dropped the hand to the tabletop and lifted his eyes. "You're a stubborn man, Thorpe—and maybe a damned fool along with it. Your wife has what folks call stomach-complaint."

Thorpe nodded his head.

"Back east," went on Doctor Nash, "it's called ulcers of the stomach. Commonly, folks get it from too much worry over a long period of time."

"By gawd, Doctor, she's worried. She's had cause to worry. We all have. We sold out down to our boots to come out here and take up this claim. And nothing's went right for us since. We're just plain slowly starving out. And that's the plain fact of it."

Doc said no more but Whit finished the last pancake, leaned back to switch his chair around until he could see the homesteader over by the old iron stove and said, "I'd like to hear the full story. Here, or down in town at the jailhouse, Mister Thorpe." His gaze ranged among the worn old dented utensils atop the stove. "You got a little coffee by any chance?"

Thorpe turned. "No sir, but we got some parched wheat we use instead and it's—"

Whit repressed a shudder. "No thanks, I'll just stay with the water." He had tasted that squatters' substitute before and it had nearly gagged him.

Poverty, he had thought the first time

he'd ever tasted that stuff, had to be the worst possible method of existence and parched wheat for coffee confirmed it.

He looked up over a troughed cigarette paper, his gaze saying all it had to say to the homesteader.

7

AN INTERESTING MORNING

When a man decided to tell the whole truth it seemed to have a purgative effect on him. The settler started out slowly, reluctantly and awkwardly, then his voice gathered strength.

"He rode in about a week back, on a big bay horse. He said his name was Smith and he'd hurt his back in a fall crossin' the mountains and was lookin' for a place where he could rest up for a few days. He offered to pay me." Thorpe gently wagged his head. "He said he was a cowboy down from up in Colorado somewhere—named a town but I don't recollect it now. I told him we didn't have any room. He pointed to the hen-house and handed me two silver dollars . . . Gents, that's the first big piece of hard money I've seen since we come out here."

Doc and Whit sat relaxed as they listened, Whit smoking, Doc just sitting.

"He didn't want no one else to know. Neither my wife nor the boy."

Whit trickled smoke. "You didn't wonder a little, Mister Thorpe?"

"Yes, I wondered. Right from the start he didn't act like anyone with a hurt in the back. But I had those two silver dollars, Marshal . . . My wife was taken with one of her bad spells. Until suppertime last night she was mostly in bed for the past few days . . . Doctor?"

Nash nodded without speaking, offering only silent confirmation of the man's statement.

"She didn't go out to the hen-house. I told the lad not to go out there neither."

"The bay horse?" asked Whit.

'The feller rode out every day before sun-up. Didn't get back mostly until after dusk. The lad didn't see him nor the horse. I think the feller watched before he rode in to make sure it'd be like that . . . I commenced to worry. He was an outlaw. I felt it in my bones as sure as I'm standin' here. He was a husky, dark feller with a little knife-scar on his chin. . . . Then he turned up missing day afore yestiddy and until last night I figured he was plumb gone. I was never so relieved in my life. Then I found that big sorrel horse in the shed with the money-pouch on him and my heart liked to stopped. I didn't want no part of whatever was goin' on so I sent the lad to Buckeye with the horse . . . and when that feller

came back last night—I figured he would
and was outside waiting—when he come
into the yard I told him—I warned him."

Doctor Nash nodded again. This too
was something he could confirm. So could
Whit, he had heard Thorpe tell the outlaw
about the horse.

"That horse didn't come up here by
himself. Someone had to bring him back
and tie him in my barn and off-saddle him.
It scairt me even worse. I figured you, Marshal, likely had done it and I worried about
why you'd done it—because you wanted to
use the sorrel horse for bait."

"And the outlaw didn't ride off," murmured Whit, who alone could offer confirmation this time—a sore neck and a small
bump under his hat. "And you knew that
too, Mister Thorpe."

The homesteader shifted position a
little before replying. "He didn't say what
he'd do, he just asked me did I have any
idea about how and when the sorrel horse

come into my barn. I told him I was surprised as hell when I went out last night,
waiting for him, and to kill time walked into
the shed and found that horse and outfit in
there."

"What did he say?"

"Nothing. Not a blessed word. He just
stood there lookin' at me. After a while he
looked around and said he wasn't going to
ride out now with maybe a posse hidin' close
by and waitin' for him to do that; he said
he'd hide out in the hen-house until late in
the night, then slip away. He told me where
he'd got that old horse and those old clothes
to make him look like another settler . . .
Then he handed me five silver dollars and
went over to the hen-house . . . That give me
seven dollars—seven silver dollars."

Whit moved his neck, which was just as
sore as ever, and said, "But he took the
sorrel horse anyway. I don't blame him. If I
figured a posse was likely to jump me any
moment I'd want power under me too."

Thorpe had one more thing to say. "Whether you catch him or not, Marshal, so help me Lord I don't never want to see that man again." He plunged a hand into one patched trouser pocket and yanked it forth, stepped to the table and dropped seven silver dollars on the oilcloth. "I don't never again want that kind of money, starvin' or not!"

Whit gazed at the dull big coins making no move to confiscate them. Then he arose. "You earned it, it's your money for givin' a room to someone. That part's all right, Mister Thorpe. But you came damned awful close to getting into something that could send you to prison for the rest of your life. Let's go, Doc . . . Mister Thorpe, take that old horse back to the squatter he was stolen from."

"Yes, sir. What'll I say about having the horse?"

Whit was dry when he responded. "You'll think of something."

Thorpe went out into the pleasant day-light with them and watched with a faint frown as they walked away southward, heads down, talking. It had not occurred to Thorpe, with all his other worries, to wonder where their mounts might be, any more than it had occurred to Turner Whit-sett to ask where that horse of his was which he had let Ulysses ride back up here from town.

By the time they were astride and heading for Buckeye Doctor Nash had turned all he had heard back there, over and over. "I don't think Thorpe was lying, Whit, but something sticks in my mind: How did that sorrel horse happen to reach Thorpe's place after he was frightened off during the gunfight?"

There were several perfectly rational answers but the lawman offered none of them. "That's part of the mystery," he told his friend. "Another part is—why didn't the outlaw get over here through the mountains the day after the robbery, instead of two days after? Doc, there are a hell of a lot of questions and right now all I care about is one of them. Where is that bastard right now?"

"In the mountains mounted on a big strong horse putting miles between him and the Buckeye territory. That's what I'd be doing."

Whit said, "Maybe," and stood in his stirrups to see whether or not he could make out rooftops yet. He couldn't.

"What do you mean—maybe?"

"Well, you been sayin' all the things you'd do if you were in that man's boots. How about the money from the pouch? You'd pretty well know where it is now, Doc, and you'd feel that you had a kind of right to it, wouldn't you?"

Doctor Nash stared. "In town . . ? Hell; he wouldn't be that foolish."

Whit shrugged. "I've never seen him. You've never seen him. He rides pretty much at night. Folks down in town wouldn't know one drifter from another." Whit showed a flinty, small smile. "That's why I said we'd ought to be heading back. I want to be around tonight, in town."

Doc frowned for a moment. "The big sorrel horse," he suddenly exclaimed. "We'd know *him.*"

"Yup, we sure would. And that bastard knows it now, because we used the horse to try and bait him. Doc, this is a clever feller. He rode right under our noses on that old nag yesterday looking like every other raggedy-assed squatter we ever saw. He's not going to ride the sorrel horse into town tonight . . . *If* he rides in tonight. He might be smarter than that, too. He might do something else."

"Such as?"

"He knew that was an army payroll pouch. If he knows this territory at all he also knows the only two posts are at Fort Hannibal and down yonder along the border. That money wasn't going to Hannibal—it was travelling *from* there—so it was meant for the Coldspring post."

Doc rode along for a while gazing out over the warming countryside before saying, "I've always felt outlaws had to be stupid. It's always seemed to me that for men to risk their lives to steal had to prove defective intellect."

"Whatever in hell that is," muttered Turner Whitsett. "As for the rest of it—you're the smart, educated man, Doc, I'm just a former rangerider who went into law work because the pay is better and the work isn't as hard. But there are smart outlaws. I've heard you say there aren't and never argued about it. I just figured that someday you'd learn otherwise. Unless you was too pig-headed to admit being a little wrong." Whit smiled, moved his head gingerly to confirm that the neck-ache was still there and said, "You want to find out whether you're right or wrong?"

Nash nodded. "How?"

"Change your clothes when we get back to town. Wear something dark. Take your shellbelt and carbine and a fresh horse and ride south of town. Maybe down about three, four miles where Apache Rocks are and get comfortable there and wait. I'll bet you a bottle of good whiskey—not Austen's usual poison—that son of a bitch will waylay the stage and take back his money-pouch. To do that, he could still use the big stout sorrel horse."

Doctor Nash scowled. "And maybe get shot by him?"

"No. Not very likely."

"The hell it's not likely. He shot his partner didn't he?"

"Yeah. Only I don't expect he'll be down there tonight. He might. He just might be down there tonight and that's the bet we're going to cover by having you down there waiting. Anyway, once you see him stop a stage you got a legal right to shoot him."

"And what'll you be doing?"

"Waiting in town, somewhere around where I can see the stage office. Maybe from up atop Austen's saloon behind the false front. Only first I aim to wander around and ask folks if they've seen a dark-lookin' stranger."

Doc snorted. "In a country full of Mexes and half-Mexes every other stranger you see is dark."

Whit did not pursue this; he yawned as they came into sight of town. The sun was almost directly overhead by now and it was just plain hot. Even in the meagre shade there was heat of the kind that made men and horses perspire while standing motion-less.

They entered from the northwest, rode down the rear alley to the livery barn, handed over their horses and walked back northward, dusty, rumpled and unshaven. A fat woman caught sight of Doctor Nash and sailed across the hot, dusty wide roadway with skirts flopping to start an irate harangue about him never being in town when he was needed. Her little Jonathan had fallen from a shed roof while trying to fly with gunnysack wings and had broken his arm.

Whit marched steadfastly onward and entered his office, went directly to the *olla* and drank until fresh perspiration popped out beneath his shirt, then went to the desk, dug out the recovered army payroll, stuffed it into his shirtfront and went up to Deacon Henderson's hot cubicle of an office.

Deacon frowned from beneath an askew green eyeshade, his expression truculent until Whit began pulling money from inside his shirt without saying a word. Then Deacon's eyes instantly widened.

Whit sat down, still without speaking, to roll and light a smoke while he waited for Deacon to finish counting. Henderson raised a pair of eyes with an expression of clear bafflement in their muddy depths.

"It's too much money, Whit."

"Nope. That's what was in the pay-roll-pouch."

"But I figured only about nine hundred."

Whit shrugged, crossed his legs and glanced out the fly-specked window. There was a very handsome woman walking northward over in front of Will Austen's saloon. She was the widow Mullaney and there was not a single man on the cow ranges or in town who had not gazed upon her with a feeling of healthy masculine longing. And a lot of men who weren't single too.

"Pretty as a spotted pony," Whit murmured.

Deacon did not even look. He ran his fingers through the money. "Are you sure this is it, Whit?"

"Yeah, I'm sure."

"Well; where is the money-pouch?"

Whit exhaled bluish smoke before replying. "It's not here. Do you want the pouch or the money?" He turned for another glance but the widow Mullaney had passed from sight. He arose. "What are you going to do with it, Deacon?"

"Stick it in another sack and get the hell rid of it. Of course. Whit—how did you recover it?"

Turner Whitsett strolled to the door to lean and look northward as he replied. "I just took it out of someone's saddlepockets . . . Deacon, why do you suppose she never re-married?"

"Who?"

"That red-headed right handsome widow woman."

"Irene Mullaney? How in hell would I know? Whit, the company's going to want to know the details of how you got this money back. And so is the army, sure as hell."

Whit sighed, pitched his cigarette stub

into the gutter and walked out into brilliant sunshine on his way over to the café.

8
WHIT'S PLAN

Somewhere that outlaw had a big bay horse. Whit had never seen it but Thorpe had and there was no doubt that he had ridden with his dead partner to the stage robbery on a good animal. Maybe he left it up near that squatter's shanty where he had stolen the old plug. And maybe he had ridden the stout sorrel back where he had left the bay and had traded horses. He knew that the sorrel would be known.

Whit sipped coffee at the café counter

staring at the pie table beyond.

There was a good chance he would do exactly as Whit had surmised; go south of town and stop the night stage, hoping that the army payroll would be on board. He might also decide the money would not be on that coach, that it would be in town. He did not know Deacon Henderson and right now disagreeable Deacon was the linchpin in this affair.

Whit put the cup down and the caféman refilled it and turned to exchange amiable insults with the dayman from the livery barn who walked in looking tired and hungry. Whit ignored them both.

The best place to stop a stage south of Buckeye was a jumble of big old grey boulders three miles south called Apache rocks because, or so legend had it anyway, rag-head marauders had ambushed a freight outfit one time.

There were other places, but Apache Rocks offered the only real shelter and protection for a good many miles southward.

He had a twinge of worry about Doctor Nash. Maybe he shouldn't have sent him down there. Doc was no gunfighter. As far as Whit knew Doc was no fighter at all, even though he had once confided that he had been in the army—as a surgeon.

On the other hand Whit could trust Doc to say nothing and there were few other men around Buckeye he had that much confidence in.

Also, Doc was no fool. He would look out for himself.

He finished the coffee, shoved forward some coins and arose feeling well fed. Outside the day was ending, but since this was summertime darkness would not arrive for several hours yet.

He was stepping up onto the opposite plankwalk when Deacon Henderson came along from the direction of the harness shop carrying some patched britchings. He said, "I wanted to ask you something, Whit.

About sending that payroll on south—the army'll be expecting it down at Coldspring, but after ponderin' on all this other trouble, I been wondering—do you think I'd ought to send it tonight or keep it in the safe for a few days until I can round up some fellers to ride shotgun with it?"

Turner Whitsett had been in this kind of situation before. A person offering advice became part of whatever ensued. If that money disappeared again, this time it would be his fault for suggesting what Henderson should do. He said, "It's up to you, Deacon. Why can't you round up some gunguards for tonight's coach?"

"There's nothing at the corralyard bunkhouse but my yardmen. Even the drivers aren't around and we only use gunguards now and then." Deacon scowled. "I tell you what I'm goin' to recommend to the company: send those damned money-pouches south to the border by the Tombstone or Lordsburg stages, or pay for a full-time gunguard to hang around down here."

Whit nodded. He knew just enough about the company Deacon worked for to know what would be said about any suggestion involving additional expense. "Are you going to send it out on the night stage, then?"

"Oh hell, I don't know. You figure that outlaw's out of the country?"

Whit answered honestly. "I wouldn't bet a plugged *centavo* on it."

Henderson's scowl deepened. "That's what I been wonderin'. If the bastard's still around . . . No, I think I'd better keep the money in the safe and post a couple of the yardmen in there all night with shotguns. And by golly, tomorrow I'm going to send up to Fort Hannibal and tell 'em I don't guarantee nothing; if they want that damned payroll to reach Coldspring to send down a cavalry escort."

Deacon would have moved along but

Whit said, "One thing, Deacon: When does the night stage pull out today?"

"Hour. Maybe a mite beyond an hour. Why?"

"I want you to do something for me— and I want you to not say a darned word about this to anyone; you understand?"

"Sure I understand. What is it?"

"Take out a bullion box, stuff a money-pouch inside it, fill the pouch with paper of some kind and when the coach's out front loading lug that box out and hand it up to the driver—in plain sight."

Henderson gazed a long time at Turner Whitsett before speaking. "You think that son of a bitch is here in town?"

"I don't know. But if he is I want him to trail after the coach—not raid your safe tonight."

Deacon gravely inclined his head. "Yeah. All right, Whit. I got faith in you. Maybe other folks don't but I do. All right."

"Not a darned word to anyone,

Deacon."

The other man grunted and paced on northward with those britchings draped over a bent arm. He looked more worried now than he had looked before. Also more grim.

Whit entered the jailhouse, rolled and lit a smoke and stood a while in thought, then went to the wallrack and took down a saddlegun, checked the magazine, dumped the gun in a boot and set it by the door. Then he returned to the roadway and thoughtfully looked up and down the roadway. Dusk was still an hour away but the sun was gone so the direct brilliance with its shimmering heat was also gone.

He went over to the general store, talked a while of minor things with the storekeeper, then went to the harness shop and did the same. He ended up along the worn barfront of Will Austen's place and because it was suppertime the bar was empty except for a bronzed, pale-looking, long-legged rangeman at the upper end drinking beer and eating a fat pickle he had fished from the pickle-jar with his pocket-knife.

Will came along looking as skeptical and doubting as ever. "Heard you recovered the stage-money," he said without sounding congratulatory.

Whit sighed to himself. That damned Deacon Henderson. If he shot his mouth about the other thing he and Whit had discussed. . . .

"Found it in some saddlepockets. How about a shot?"

Will went to get the bottle. He brought back two glasses. As they sipped warm whisky Austen recalled a robbery from years back, before Whit's time. It had occurred right in the centre of town. "In broad daylight, mind you," he exclaimed. "Those dumb damned fools didn't even get to the end of town. It was like shooting sage-hens."

Whit had heard this story at least a dozen times. It rarely came out differently so this had to be about how it had happened.

The whisky did nothing for him on a full stomach so he re-filled the glass. Will did the same. He rarely drank with customers; in fact he did not drink very much at all. Once he'd told Whit that every shot-glassfull a barman consumed cut the profit down just that much.

"Whose saddlepockets?" he asked, when he thought a discreet period of time had passed, and Whit smiled at him.

"Not yours, so you don't have to worry, Will."

Austen must have expected a rebuke of some kind. He passed it off. "Deacon said it was an army payroll. Good thing it was recovered. Otherwise we'd have soldiers all over Buckeye by next week."

"You'd do all right," replied Whit dryly, shoving his glass aside and fishing for some silver to pay for his drinks.

"Yeah, I would for a fact. Years ago when they were ridin' patrol during the rag-head troubles and while them Messican *pornunciados* was forever sneakin' up here to steal horses for their raggedy-pantsed rebel armies, we used to have some pretty big detachments camp out back of town, and by golly I did a business them days."

"No soldiers nowadays," murmured Whit, "and not many strangers either, eh?"

"Hasn't been a soldier ride in here by golly in several years, for a fact. And strangers—now and then, during the riding season, mostly."

"Any today?"

Austen shook his head. "Today? Hell, hasn't been anything but a gang of freighters in a couple of weeks."

Whit smiled and departed. He had led up to this same question in every business establishment he had visited over the past hour, so if the outlaw was around he was not being very conspicuous.

Whit went out back into the littered alleyway and used the fire-ladder nailed to the rear of Austen's building to climb up. To reach the false-front atop the building next door he only had to cross Austen's roof and step across a two-foot dogtrot.

It was hotter up there but visibility was excellent despite the fading daylight. He could see for several miles in all directions. In one place someone was driving a bunch of cattle or a band of horses. Dust rose and steadily moved. Otherwise he did not even see a wagon-camp, which would have been common-place this time of year when freighters worked steady runs between the south desert and the northerly towns and ranges.

He did not really expect to see someone riding a big stout sorrel horse coming at a leisurely gait toward town, but it would have simplified things. He mopped sweat. Life was an experience where not many easy answers cropped up.

He knelt in shade which was almost as hot as it would have been if the sun had still been up there, willing just to be motionless and quiet. That second jolt of Will Austen's whisky had left him feeling slightly buoyant but the longer he squatted up there looking in all directions the more he sweated out all the pleasantness.

By the time he was ready to give up, Deacon Henderson was out front profanely supervising the parking of a four-up hitch and a faded old stagecoach out front of the corralyard.

There were a lot of new stagecoaches but they never appeared on the south desert. There was little traffic, some light freight and less money down here. When coaches looked bad in other towns they were replaced with new outfits and the old ones wound up in places like Buckeye.

He watched the coach being checked and fussed over, watched the whip with his elegant smoke-tanned grey gauntlets saunter from the office, his baton of office in one hand—a handsome, highly-polished, long whip in one hand. There were sterling ferrules at intervals up the whip.

The driver was an older man. No doubt years back he had been a genuine knight of the road; otherwise he would not have that beautiful silvered whip. But like old horses and old stages, old drivers too ended up pushing through acrid desert dust on runs self-respecting drivers would not accept.

Whit arose, sighed and turned to cross back to the fire-ladder and climb down. What he had in mind, had in fact planned to do since he and Doctor Nash had returned from the Thorpe homestead, had to be either done now or abandoned. One way, he was taking a hell of a chance. The other way he would be taking almost no chance—and he was probably not going to catch his outlaw either.

If he had been older, or perhaps if his

spirit and character had been different, he would have chosen the least hazardous of his alternatives. He had a couple of weak moments even then, as he crossed through the dogtrot to his office, opened the door and reached around for the Winchester in the boot he had placed there an hour or so before, but as soon as he had the gun he felt the resolve stiffen.

He went out back, walked briskly down to the lower end of town, walked past the livery barn and public corrals, down among the shacks and shanties of Mex faggot-gatherers, got past the last of them and where the road made a slight dogleg in order to get around ancient *jacals* which had been there since before Buckeye had been a full-fledged community he slackened his pace. He listened for the jangle of old chain harness, then walked up to the edge of the road and stood, booted carbine slung indifferently over a shoulder, waiting.

The stage came with slack harness and

sagging single-trees because there was an ordinance against busting out of town. Too much dust was raised, too many chickens had been run over and folks didn't care whether some whip wanted to make a flourishing exit or not.

Whit saw the vehicle sag around the dogleg, saw the whip raise his snappers to make the customary pistol-shot crack over the leaders' heads and casually raised a hand.

The whip hung motionless for a moment, then gradually lowered his gauntleted right hand to grasp lines with both hands and shove a big boot to the brake-binder as he soothed his horses down to a halt.

Whit smiled up, flung open the door and as the driver irritably said, "Marshal; most folks get in back at the yard," Whit kept smiling and climbed in.

The driver whistled up his horses and walked them for a full half mile before unfurling the whip. Strong horses hitting collars jerked a stage forward with the impact of a bucking horse. There were two other passengers inside with Turner Whitsett, both peddlers with sample-cases. They were braced, so evidently they had ridden this run before. Whit shoved the booted Winchester against the opposite seat. Even so the shock was rough and battering. One of the peddlers swore in a tone of voice full of resignation and disgust, the way a passenger would react when there were no ladies aboard, when he had been abused like this on board stagecoaches most of his mature life. The other travelling man simply re-set his little Derby hat and waggled his head in phlegmatic acceptance of one of the unavoidable evils of life.

Whit knew neither of them. They knew him only by the badge of his shirtfront and that was no novelty, so after that fearful bucking had turned to the pitching and swaying of a stagecoach being pulled by galloping horses, one of the travelling salesmen said in a very loud voice, "That gun, Marshal—you're not expecting trouble, I hope?"

Whit shook his head, then gazed out the window on his left to see how far they had come. About a mile and a half. He settled the booted Winchester between his knees.

If that damned outlaw hit Henderson's safe tonight, while Whit was taking this wild gamble, Whit was going to look awfully bad to the townsmen for not being in town.

But if Deacon had two men in there with shot guns . . . He turned to watch as one of the peddlers produced a deck of cards and invited the other salesman to join in a game of blackjack.

The shadows which fell elsewhere at this late time of day did not arrive on the south desert. Perhaps the heat had something to do with it. At any rate, the entire world down here just continued to shade off from light grey to deeper grey and eventually to smoky-dusk and finally, about nine o'clock, darkness dropped like a sudden shroud.

The heat lingered, but people who had spent years in the country west of Texas and east of California, in that long, arid strip of land which no one had ever really wanted but which had been fought over because it gave access to better areas, accepted heat as they accepted daily thirst; it was something to be borne and after enough years on the south desert a man's blood got thin enough so that if he went north, into Colorado or Wyoming, for example, even in mid-summer when the days are pleasant but the nights were cold he suffered.

Turner Whitsett was comfortable. The coach stirred a slight, breathless breeze and that helped a little. He thought of rolling a smoke but gave it up. The road was rutted and rough and he really did not feel much urge anyway.

Those peddlers held their cards with

both hands and had the spare ones propped upon the seat between their two Derby hats. It was a hell of a way to play cards but maybe to them anything was better than just sitting there being bumped and bruised.

They were getting close to Apache Rocks. Whit leaned, without his hat, and looked southward. The rocks loomed darkly in an arc-wide jumble. In later years people would speculate, when folks had more leisure time to do such things, how those huge granite boulders had got there. There was not another rock of that kind for a hundred miles in any direction. Whit's interest had never been in the origin of those rocks, or any other rocks, and now as he squinted through the dusk he paid less heed to the boulders than he did to the countryside around them. Doc was out there somewhere. Unless he had changed his mind at the last moment, which Whit doubted very much. What Whit wanted to be certain of was that Doc had not left his horse in sight. Evidently he hadn't because the land was empty, totally deserted in appearance.

Whit pulled his head back. If the outlaw was in those rocks, fine, if not, if he was elsewhere farther along, Whit was going to be there too. But if he was back in Buckeye, then Whit was going to ride this coach all the way to its stop at Coldspring and return tomorrow—and probably ride into a town upset enough to hang him and certainly angry enough to fire him.

He pulled his head back in, raised the saddleboot containing his carbine to the crook of one arm and bounced along— waiting.

9

DANGER!

The driver slackened gait after a while with Apache Rocks to the rear a mile and allowed his horses to cool out as nightfall steadily settled and the peddlers finished their game of blackjack. One of them had lost two bits, which was not a lot of money, and they settled back to discuss business. Neither of them paid the slightest attention to the lawman with his booted Winchester.

Whit was beginning to have a bad feeling. The best thing now would be for that outlaw to be out of the country and it was a possibility. He was almost prepared to hope this in fact was the way things would work out when the driver sang down to his horses and the coach began braking down to a halt.

Whit looked out. Nightfall was close; there was still fair visibility for a mile or so but it would not last much longer. He leaned to look ahead but the horses impeded vision as they came down to a shuffling walk and finally to a halt. It was the kind of halt a driver would make if something were wrong with his hitch or his vehicle and Whit had no inkling it was not something like this until the coach stopped and he shoved open the door to step out.

The driver leaned and spoke in a quiet voice. "Marshal. . . ."

Whit glanced up. There were two of them up there, the grey, grizzled driver and a thick-shouldered dark man with a cocked Colt aimed squarely at Whit's chest.

The surprise was perfect.

The driver did not seem too upset as he looped his lines around the brake-handle and kept both gauntleted hands in plain sight.

The dark man's voice was sharper than the driver's voice had been. The driver had sounded resigned but not especially fearful. The other man's words hit the warm night air like steel balls striking glass.

"Shuck the gun, Marshal, and step away from the coach."

Whit knew who the dark man was without wasting time guessing. He tossed his six-gun down and walked backwards a couple of yards.

"You other two inside there," called the outlaw, "climb out hands in front and empty. *Move!*"

Both peddlers hunched over and stepped out upon the same side. Whit felt like swearing; why the hell hadn't they climbed out the opposite door, that would have forced the highwayman to look away from Whit.

The driver talked to his horses when they fidgeted. He calmed them and turned his head slowly to exchange a look with Turner Whitsett. He seemed reproachful, as though this were the lawman's fault.

The outlaw ordered both peddlers to shed their coats, which they did, and neither had a gunbelt beneath so the outlaw turned his attention back to Whit. "Walk down in front of the lead team, Marshal. Stay out a few feet so I can keep an eye on you."

Whit obeyed. For the first time, now that the surprise had passed, he began to feel relieved. The son of a bitch hadn't stayed in town after all. When Whit faced around he was expressionless.

The outlaw hoisted the bullion box and heaved it over the side. He accomplished this one-handed. When the box struck he turned and gestured for the whip to climb down. The older man had been awaiting instructions and complied without haste or without resentment. He had probably done this or something like it fifty times in his years as a stage-driver and he was still alive so he had evidently done it properly.

The outlaw motioned them all up where Whit was standing. He waited, then he too climbed down but on the far side and using only one hand to hold with. When he was on the ground he stepped over the bullion box and walked up to halt beside the far-side leader. The horse eyed him with the same expression of resigned expectation the driver had been showing. The horse, like the driver, was prepared to do whatever was required of him because he had no choice and that was the end of it. He neither approved nor disapproved, he simply waited.

The pair of salesmen watched that dark man with the gun the way they would have watched a coiled rattlesnake. Whit was standing easy, arms hanging; the salesmen

both had their hands chest high, palms forward.

The outlaw showed no emotion as he
said, "You're goin' to walk, gents." He then
stepped back to loosen the tugs, pull down
the lines until he could unbuckle them,
looped each line around a hame,
unsnapped the tongue to the leaders and
freed each horse from its mate; then he led
them forward and clucked. The horses were
bewildered and only walked a few paces,
then looked back, but the outlaw was
freeing the second hitch in the same way.
When he had them all off the tongue he
picked up a handful of gravel and flung it.
The horses moved away, then trotted, dragging their traces. One of them, younger
than the others, decided he was indeed free
and broke over into a gallop.

Whit sighed. That would be all it would
take. He was correct; the other three horses
finally decided they could run too.

As the animals awkwardly loped out

down the roadway the outlaw wiped horse-sweat off one hand down his pants' leg and stood back by the disabled coach studying his prisoners. "Stay here, gents, and don't get any fancy ideas. I'll be watching."

He moved off, grasped a handle of the bullion box and began backing down the far side of the coach but out far enough to be able to see the four stationary figures up ahead in the roadway. Finally the driver said, "Where in hell's he got a horse tied around here? There ain't even any decent buckbrush to tie one to."

One of the peddlers spoke from the side of his mouth in a conspiratorial whisper. "He don't know about that carbine, Marshal."

Whit said nothing. He too had been wondering where the outlaw had his horse. They were down upon a barren, gritty stretch of desert where what little underbrush existed hugged the ground no higher than sage. But it was nightfall, and no doubt the outlaw had planned it this way. He had a horse somewhere around, that was a fact, and maybe the animal was hobbled because it did not have to be tied to anything if the man had brought along a pair of hobbles.

Whit turned to see where those harness-horses had got to. They had stopped loping so they were probably not too far off but he could not discern them in the settling night. As he turned back a sudden gunshot broke the desert hush. Both the peddlers fell face down as though they had been shot.

A second gunshot sounded, then in swift order two more, one from a handgun, loud and throaty, the second one from a carbine, sharper, more flat and distinct.

Whit ran to the near side of the coach and lunged past the ajar door, shook loose the boot and stepped quickly to the high rear wheel with his carbine.

There was no more gunfire. He thought it had come from both sides of the roadway, the carbine to the west, the hand-gun fire from the east, but that was a guess. One thing which seemed certain was that the outlaw had not fired the carbine. He'd only had a six-gun during the robbery. If he'd reached his horse, though, he would undoubtedly have a Winchester slung under the *rosadero.*

Silence re-settled deeper than before as Whit speculated. Those men up front of the coach had moved closer to it for protection. He heard the imperturbable driver say, "Just quit shakin' gents; I think whatever it was is about over with."

Whit had been wondering along these lines too. One way or the other it seemed to be over.

A man called from northward. "You fellers by the stagecoach—you all right?"

Whit's grip on the carbine loosened in surprise. Doc Nash! "Yeah, we're all right.

Where is the son of a bitch, Doc?"

"Gone," Doc replied laconically. "But not for long."

Whit started walking back up the road, carbine slung in the crook of one arm. Where they met Doc said, "I thought that was you looking out the window up by Apache Rocks. You had your hat off which made it easy to recognise you. I thought you were going to hang around town."

Whit smiled. "Got to worryin' about you being out here and figured someone had better come baby-sit you." He looked around and Doc pointed. "Yonder's the bullion box. Come here, I want to show you something."

It was dark but there was no mistaking what Doc pointed to. Blood on the box. Doc sounded surprised when he said, "I hit him, by golly."

"You trailed the stage?" Whit asked, leaning low to feel the blood.

"Yes. When I knew you were aboard it I

wondered if perhaps you hadn't come up with something; maybe you knew where he would hit."

Whit straightened up shaking his head. "It was a guess. And for a while I thought it was a bad one, too." He turned as the stage-driver came walking up. He handed Whit a six-gun. "Yours, Marshal," he said and glanced past at the box, then looked at Doctor Nash. "You fellers must have set this up some way," he said in that same, imperturbable, almost inflectionless tone of voice he had used throughout the robbery.

Whit had one question. "How did that son of a bitch happen to be up there with you, mister?"

The older man pointed back toward the coach. "He jumped into the boot, he told me, a half mile below town—after you'd got aboard, Marshal, and rode back there until he was down about where he stopped us. Then he climbed over the top of the coach and the first thing I knew someone tapped me on the shoulder and when I looked around there was a gun in my face." The driver turned politely aside to expectorate, then turned back. "Ain't you the doctor from up at Buckeye?" he asked.

Adrian Nash, leaning on his Winchester and knowing exactly how the driver's thoughts were running, smiled at the older man. "I chase outlaws when the doctoring business is slack," he said.

Whit had a fresh problem. The only saddle animal belonged to Nash. He had no right to commandeer it but he and Doc could not make much headway in pursuit riding double either.

The driver seemed to settle this problem almost indifferently when he said, "Marshal, that young horse, the one that taken the others off in a lope, he's broke to ride. In fact he was a ridin' horse when Henderson bought him and put him in harness—if you was thinkin' of goin' after that feller."

Doc hoisted his Winchester. "I'll get my

animal if he didn't run all the way back to Buckeye when that shooting started—and see if I can round up the harness-horses." He hung there briefly gazing at Whit. "You want to go after him in the dark?"

"If he's hit, Doc, it would only be the decent thing to do."

Doc continued to look at his friend. "I'm sure that's your only motivation, Marshal," he said, and turned away.

The driver looked after Nash. "Nice feller," he said in that calm, deep and laconic voice of his. "But he sure uses big words, don't he?"

Whit picked up the bullion box and carried it back to the stage, flung it inside and as the driver started to say it had ought to be up front with him Whit explained.

"It's empty. There's a money-pouch in it stuffed with newspapers." Before the whip could speak again Whit also said, "Can you make it on down to Coldspring with three horses?"

This was something the driver knew all about. "I could make it with just two horses as long as I take my time and don't have no more weight aboard than I'll have from here on . . . You sure that box is empty? Deacon Henderson told me to keep it under my feet all the time and be right careful with it."

Whit smiled. "It's empty," he said and turned to watch Doctor Nash lope past with an upraised hand in salute. The pair of travelling men looked from the dark-clad sinister horse-man to the lawman, their degree of bewilderment increasing rather than decreasing.

Whit rolled a smoke finally and tried to imagine where a wounded outlaw would go in this open, barren, southerly territory where there was not even enough water to keep a goat alive and, while it was dark now, when dawn came, wherever he had got to, he would still be without shelter.

BLOOD!

Whit led the harness-horse even after they found where the outlaw had left his hobbled horse but even so it was difficult to keep the tracks in sight, soft, gritty ground notwithstanding.

Doctor Nash was of the opinion they would be doing something great if they covered two miles all night long, and Whit's answer to that was basic.

"Two miles is better than nothing and the other thing we could do is sit out here swapping lies until daylight."

They finally decided the outlaw was riding straight east. His tracks had been pointing in that direction for about an hour without deviating when Whit turned and vaulted upon the bare back of the harness-horse. Just for a moment the horse bunched up. If he had bucked Whit would have gone sailing. He had nothing, no saddle, not even a circingle. But he hauled the horse around and growled at him, getting in his bluff first, and the horse lined out.

Doc said, "There's a goat ranch out here, but southward, closer to the border, and it's quite a few miles yet. Otherwise I've never seen anything but rocks and gila monsters, scorpions and snakes down here."

What puzzled Whit was the route of the fleeing man. If he had turned southward he at least would have been riding in the direction of the border and, if he managed to stay astride that long, once he got across no U.S. lawman could go after him.

At least that was the law; international law but not always south-desert law. Whit had brought them back from down there but it usually been done at night like a skulking Apache or if it had been in broad daylight it had cost him anywhere from five to twenty dollars U.S. The *rurales* who patrolled the lower side of the line had no love for *gringos* with badges or without them but they had a great respect for U.S. greenbacks, which were one-to-fifty with Mex double-eagles.

Eventually that idea occurred to Doctor Nash too. "Why straight east? Why not south across the line?"

Whit gave the only answer he had come up with. "Because somewhere out here to the east he's got a hideout. Or maybe a friend."

Doc was doubtful about both. This was flat desert; a hideout to be worth anything would have to blend with the countryside: with trees or rocks or arroyos or bluffs and there were none of those things for a hundred and more miles.

"Can you find that goat ranch in the dark?" Whit asked.

Doc was confident. "Yes, but it's south, not east."

"Maybe he'll change course."

They almost bypassed a place where a shred of soiled white made Doc's horse bow its neck and softly blow. They turned.

Doc stepped off, picked up the scrap of cloth, examined it and without a word handed it to Whit. There was sticky dark blood on it.

They rode on.

If the outlaw had had to stop and tear up his shirt to make a bandage he was hurt badly enough.

Then Whit climbed off and rubbed his rear. That stage-company horse may have been a saddle animal and maybe he was pretty fair in harness but he had the boniest back Whit had ever straddled, even as a kid when he'd always ridden bareback because he had not owned a saddle.

Doc was solicitous. "The old-timers told me Indians used to fill their britches with sage when they rode razorback horses."

Whit stopped rubbing. "It's a darned lie. Mostly they didn't even own any britches with a seat in them and when they got a pair they cut the seat out."

He walked ahead again, leading the bony-backed horse. The tracks were not difficult to see once they got on the trail although by daylight they could certainly have made much better time.

Then they began curving southward and as soon as Doctor Nash noticed that Whit was angling away on a new course he said, "I thought so. I've been betting on it for the past hour. He's heading for that goat ranch."

"Or the border," stated Whit without taking his eyes off the ground. "Over here the boundary line veers northward considerably."

They halted when one of the horses hung back. A moment later the other horse also reacted to something. Whit said, "Water."

He was correct. They let the horses have their heads and were led to a little spring where the only trees they had seen all night stood, stunted but green, in a gravelly place with rip-gut grass stirrup-high and some tall, flourishing paloverdes delicately spreading from their fragile tops like umbrellas.

The water had a faint taste of sulphur and after Doc tanked up his horse and also drank he gravely said, "Naturally; this is Dante's purgatory isn't it?"

Whit did fall into that trap. There was no one named Dante that he knew of, anyway, who lived on the south desert. He

was not going to let Doc make him the butt
of a joke.

"He don't know this country too well,
Doc, or he'd have come over here for
water."

Doc was unconvinced of this. "That
goat ranch is only about three miles from
here."

They took a chance, abandoned the
tracks and rode directly for the goat ranch.

Whit did not know the place until he
saw the buildings, low, thick, made by
hands with some skill, no knowledge of
construction and lots of time, then he
remembered having been past here a time
or two years earlier. At that time, if he
recalled correctly, the place had been abandoned. Now, despite the lateness, there was
a lingering aroma of woodsmoke in the still,
heavy atmosphere.

"Old Mex and his daughter," murmured Doc as they sat their horses out a
short distance. "For the life of me I can't

imagine why anyone would want to live out
here."

"You've treated him?"

"No. The daughter. The first time a rattlesnake bit her on the foot. She had a leg as
big as a flour sack by the time they got her
up to town. The last time was about seven
or eight months ago. Scorpion got her a
good lick that time. Her name is Eulalia. I
asked her finally why she didn't move up to
Buckeye. She said her father loved his
goats." Doc fished inside his coat and found
a cigar which he lighted inside his hat to
hide the match-flare.

Whit watched, then said, "Doc, if I
didn't know you better I'd say you've been
on a few backtrails yourself. Lightin' the
stogie behind your hat. Pickin' off that son
of a bitch right after the robbery."

Nash's white teeth showed in a wide
smile. "You've been at your trade too long,
Whit. Well; do we ride right on in?"

"I take it back, you never were an

outlaw or by now you'd be dead. We ride into that yard and if he's down there he'll blow our heads off."

"Then what do we do?"

"You," stated the marshal, "stay out here and mind this bony-backed wolf-bait for me while I sneak around down there and see if there's a freshly ridden *caballo* in a corral." Whit sniffed. "Yeah, they got goats. This'll be my second go-round with goats since we've been after this man."

The night was bland but cooling, which meant it was wearing along towards another dawn. The stars offered some light, enough for those ancient buildings to show ghost-like on Whit's right as he walked ahead.

There was more browse down here but very little tall underbrush. At the old buildings three giant cottonwood trees loomed high and thick and shiny green to make pale silhouettes with their light-coloured trunks in an atmosphere which otherwise was dark and brooding.

The Indians maintained that those old abandoned adobes were all haunted. Looking at this set of old structures now, Whit could understand someone thinking something like that.

There was even a feeling of haunted-ness. He felt it but was not bothered by it and when he was close enough to be able to make out windows and doors he could also hear some goats making little sounds behind the faggot fence north of a roofless old adobe which may have been a residence once but which now, no longer protected by three-foot eaves and a roof, was being slowly washed away by south-desert infre-quent rainfalls, which when they arrived were usually veritable deluges.

He worried about a dog. Or perhaps a pack of them. Mexican goatherders were as bad as Indians for keeping alert, suspicious, treacherous dogs. So Whit waited a long while for his scent to precede him.

If there was a dog, or more than one dog, they either slept like stones or were corralled inside somewhere and could not detect strange scents. Or maybe they were lying in ambush, waiting for him to come closer.

He circled around, got north of that faggot corral, then, using it as shelter as long as possible, got right down to it and here the goat-smell was almost overpowering. No wonder if there were dogs they hadn't been able to pick up his scent.

He found two horses in a smaller, second faggot corral and got up close to find a place where he could see through. One of those horses was a big bay with drying sweat clearly visible on his neck, flanks, ribs and up where a saddle had pressed the hair flat. He was eating. The other horse was much older and indifferent to the presence of the bay. He had one of the most swayed backs Whit had ever seen. He guessed this old grey to be close to thirty.

There was a two-wheeled *carreta* beside a shed with no door and not even rawhide over the square window holes. If this was how the old Mex had got his daughter up to Buckeye no wonder her leg had been as big as a flour sack.

Something moved in the darkness near the tongue of the cart and Whit had his holstered Colt in his fingers in two seconds.

There *was* a dog. He was sleeping, stretching mightily without opening his eyes; then he went slack again. Whit waited a long while before he could make out enough grey around the eyes and muzzle to realise that this dog was very old. Maybe he had detected strange man-scent and maybe not but in either case it was not being allowed to interfere with his sleep.

A faint sound came from the *jacal* southwest of the shed. Whit waited for the sound to be repeated and when it came again he debated his course, decided to go back for Doc, moved away from where the old dog was lying, got around behind the faggot corral and turned to briskly trot.

Doc was on the ground holding their horses, still smoking his cigar and as Whit came up and said, "Tie 'em, Doc. I think we got him down there," Doctor Nash turned at once to find a suitable bush to tether his animal to.

He lifted out his carbine. It was on the tip of Whit's tongue to tell him he would not need a long-gun but in the end as they started forward, circling out and around as Whit had done earlier in order to have the shelter of the goat-corral, Whit lost all interest in whether or not his companion had brought along a Winchester.

They took their time and got down to where they could see the main *jacal,* then Whit turned off from his earlier route in order to avoid the old dog and they approached the *jacal* from the west. Here, finally, Whit saw a sliver of light. Someone had draped an ancient, mothy old blanket

over a window. Through one diagonal rip
the candle-glow showed but it was too weak
to be visible much beyond the yard.

Doc spat out his cigar and stepped
upon it, stepped ahead to Whit's left and
halted beside a boxed-in well or spring
where a wooden bucket hung suspended
from a frayed old lariat rope which was
secured to an overhead log-beam.

Whit got closer, palmed his six-gun,
took a final step to approach that shrouded
window and saw someone in pale cloth pick
up a basin and cross before the rip in the
blanket heading for the door. Whit had
barely time to turn and frantically gesture
for Doc to get down out of sight before the
door opened on its leather hinges and
someone walked forth. If he had looked he
would have sighted Turner Whitsett flat-
tened against the adobe wall. Instead, he
went with a long, business-like stride over
toward the well.

For Doctor Nash, in a low crouch, there

was no possible way to escape detection. He waited as long as he dared, then unwound and cocked his carbine in one motion.

The person with the basin seemed turned to stone. It was a woman, full-bodied with a broad, low forehead and a face which showed total astonishment as she freed one hand from the basin and raised it to her mouth.

Doc softly said, "Not a sound, *Sénorita*. Not one sound!"

Whit held his breath, certain the woman would scream. When she didn't he stepped away from the house, looked once towards the ajar old door, then walked up behind her. She heard him but did not take her black gaze off Doctor Nash. Not even when Whit stepped around to one side where she could see him.

When Whit spoke, though, she turned slightly. "Who's hurt in the house?"

She kept one hand to her heavy, handsome mouth without making any attempt to reply. She stared almost fixedly at the badge on Whit's shirt.

Doc spoke softly to her. "*Señorita* Costanso—who is in there with your father?"

Her hand came down slowly. "You almost frightened me to death," she murmured, turning back to face the doctor. "What are you doing out here—so late in the night?"

Doc eased the carbine-barrel down. "*Señorita*—who is he!"

She still had not completely recovered. She turned once more to look at Turner Whitsett's hatbrim-shadowed, lean face. "A stranger," she muttered.

"Shot?" asked Whit and she slowly nodded at him.

"*Si, Señor.* He rode in an hour ago and fell off the horse. We were in bed. My father heard the noise and came out with a candle." She turned back facing Doctor

Nash. "He needs you, Doctor."

Nash nodded but Whit had a question for the handsome woman. "How did he happen to ride here, *Señorita?*"

She shrugged sturdy shoulders. "You may ask him, *jefe.*" Now, finally, the full shock at being stopped by a pair of armed men in the pit of the night at her well-box passed. She even reached to lower the bucket until it fell into water some distance below. Doctor Nash leaned aside the Winchester to gallantly crank the bucket up and set it to one side so she could fill the basin from it.

She neither thanked him nor looked up again until the basin had been filled, then she straightened around facing Marshal Whitsett.

"You shot him, *jefe?*"

Whit shook his head and moved slightly to allow her to proceed in the direction of the *jacal.* "Is he armed, lady?"

She gave Whit a look of almost pure

scorn. "*Señor,* see for yourself, he cannot even hold a gun let alone lift one. Yes, he was armed, but my father put the gun on a table." She continued to regard Whit with an expression of near-scorn, then stepped past to lead the way. She halted near the door.

Whit still had his six-gun in his right fist. He gestured for her to enter and as she turned to do so Whit turned to Doc and pointed to that blanketed window. Without a word Doc turned and stepped over there as Whit ducked his head and entered the *jacal.*

Their precaution, however, was unnecessary. Even in the feeble light Whit saw the moment he entered the low-ceilinged room that the man lying on the pallet over along the east wall was not aware that anyone at all was in the room, not even the old white-headed man who was leaning over him with a clean rag.

11

TOWARD A NEW DAY

The old Mexican turned to accept that basin of water from his daughter, stared for a moment behind her where Whit was standing, then turned back to the man on the pallet as though seeing a stranger, an armed lawman, standing in the gloom of the small room had not startled him. Maybe it hadn't.

Whit stepped closer, stood beside the handsome woman with the black hair and eyes and the creamy skin and peered.

The outlaw's upper body was bare; his skin was lighter where it had been protected from the elements but his hands and wrists, his face and neck, were much darker.

What held Turner Whitsett's attention was the wound. It was a tiny purplish hole with the blood oozing slowly as the old man mopped it off with his wet rag. Whit knew one thing—this man was not going to see dawnlight. He straightened back and turned toward the window beyond which Doctor Nash was standing. He jerked his head.

Doc entered and moved over beside the pallet. The old man ignored him until Doc leaned to brush light fingers over the area of the wound and then to ask in soft Spanish if the bullet had exited. The old Mexican still did not look around but he answered.

"Yes. The wound is larger out the back."

Doc straightened up looking at the solitary candle. To the handsome woman he said, "It's not very good light."

She moved immediately to get another candle. She lit two more in fact and placed them near where Doc was standing.

The old man was dark, perhaps because his hair was nearly white and also perhaps because in this poor light there was no chance for any of them to appear very pale. He shuffled back a step or two in order for Doctor Nash to have more room and he softly said, "It is of no use," his Spanish different from most border-Spanish.

Whit placed him immediately. Not all border Mexicans were in fact *Mexicans;* there was a minority of what were called *criollos* nowadays but which in other times had been called *Gachupínes,* which actually simply meant that they were people who wore spurs—an idiomatic term for Spaniards; a term used now as a form of derision and dislike but in earlier times used to denote descendants of the conquering Spanish. This old man and his handsome buxom daughter were of pure

Spanish descent—*criollos*. They were Mexicans only in the sense that they could have been born in Mexico or at least in territories which had once belonged to Mexico. They were not as a rule liked by real Mexicans. Many of them lived as these people lived—apart from Mexicans who seldom missed an opportunity to humiliate them and also from the *gringos* who lumped all people of the south desert and *Mejico* as Mexicans, disliking and distrusting all of them.

Whit watched the woman's soft profile. She was beautiful. Full and mature and truly beautiful but there was a set variety of astringency around her heavy mouth which showed purpose and resolve. She was not a weak individual. He shifted his attention to the old man. Neither the father nor the daughter seemed to remember Whit was also in the gloomy little room.

The old man was slightly stooped and taller than most Mexicans and had the settled look of age and resignation. If he was the woman's father then either she was older than she looked or she was the off-spring of his later years because Whit guessed the man to be close to seventy while the woman did not seem to him to be more than thirty. At the most thirty-five.

He was darker than she was, but that happened often; men were subjected to far more sunlight and weather than women if they lived in the country.

It slowly dawned on Whit that the dying outlaw had the colouring which was mid-way between the beautiful woman and the old man. He returned his attention to the outlaw, watched Doc work bending over, sure hands doing what could be done for this man Doc had shot, and saw the faint though persevering likeness. He let his breath out slowly and reached to touch the woman's arm and jerk his head. She duti-fully followed him out into the paling late night where at long last a faint coolness was noticable. She halted, arms folded, looking steadily at him, giving the impression that whatever life brought before her she faced head-on.

His border-Spanish was adequate but these people were purists. Fine Spanish as a language was about all they had left. He spoke in English when he said, "The stranger—he just rode in and fell off his horse?"

She studied his face from candid black eyes and nodded.

He had never been a very tactful individual although right now he wished he had been. "*Señorita,* I have a rule when I talk to folks. I try never to force them to lie." He let that lie between for a moment before also saying, "He's no stranger."

She did not show any expression. Nor did she answer his implication for a while. Finally she swung partly to glance in the direction of the well-box. In accentless English she said, "He is my brother."

Whit had guessed this. "I don't think he will live until morning."

Very quietly she agreed. "No, I don't think he will either." Then she turned back, arms still folded across her chest. "I have no tears left, *jefe*."

Whit understood. "He killed a man—another outlaw. He robbed a stagecoach north of Buckeye. He stopped another coach south of town and got shot and came over here . . . Whatever I can do, I will do."

She kept gravely studying him. "I knew who you were when you came up behind me at the spring. I've seen you before. In Buckeye."

He didn't remember ever having seen her before and now, looking at her in the soft pre-dawn, he was certain that if he had ever seen her before he surely would have remembered.

"What could you do, *jefe?* What could anyone do?"

"Well; a decent burial?"

"No. We will bury him out here." She
seemed to relent just a trifle though. "*Gra-
cias*. Will you tell me how it happened?"

He wouldn't, not as long as Doc was in
their house, and in fact this was a subject he
never discussed, least of all with next-of-
kin.

"*Señorita* . . . what good would it do?"

She looked him squarely in the eye. She
knew exactly what he was doing. "No good.
You are right, it would do no good. When a
man dies—he just dies." She glanced briefly
in the direction of the house then back. "He
was my father's only son. He was a grown
man, a *vaquero* for the big cow outfits, when
I was a little girl. My father was proud—for
a while. Even afterwards, when he saw his
son's picture on posters, he said it was justified; that he only stole from *gringos* and
they had stolen our land anyway."

"And . . . ?"

"My father is a very honest man, *jefe*.
He stopped talking about my brother.

Would not answer when I mentioned him. It was a dull knife turning slowly through his heart."

"I'm very sorry."

She let her arms fall to her sides; she was finally relaxed in his company. "I stood with a candle tonight before you came, thinking the Good Lord at least let him come back to die with us; thinking that the Good Lord knew it was time for all the badness to end but He would let him come back one more time."

Whit saw her full mouth tighten. She was fighting back her agony. He wanted to say something but nothing which came to mind seemed to fit and he was wise enough then to say nothing at all.

She started to turn, then paused to look up at him again. "I don't blame you at all."

He watched her return to the house. Around him a fresh day was arriving very slowly and fragrantly in the heartland of the lower south-desert. Creosote bush and catclaw, faint moisture on cottonwood leaves and curing sparse goat-grass, blended into the unique fragrance of the desert. It was a scent duplicated nowhere else.

He rolled and lit a cigarette and because he did not want to return to the house he walked out, found their horses and brought them in to be watered at the spring, then tied them without their bridles and with loosened cinches.

The goats were restless inside their faggot corral. Evidently the old man took them out each day in the dewy early morning to browse, then perhaps returned with them before the fierce heat arrived.

Whit saw the bay horse standing head-to-tail with that sway-backed ancient grey, drowsing, and finally when the old dog awakened and saw a stranger he struggled up onto all four legs and growled but he wobbled when he started to move.

Whit knelt and slowly reached out, then scratched the old dog's back. They became instant friends. The old dog's eyes watered and he faintly wagged a matted old thinning tail. He seemed to have moments when he remembered things. Twice he gathered himself as though for a duty, looking toward the faggot corral. But his span of attention was very brief and moments later he looked at Whit, forgetting entirely whatever it was which had held his attention.

Doc came out, stretched, lifted his hat and scratched, then re-set the hat and walked over to sit on the edge of the water-box and gaze at his hands.

Whit sauntered over. "Dead?"

Doc nodded, flexed his fingers and looked up. "That's the first time I ever killed a man."

"They don't know it was you. As far as I'm concerned they'll never know. I told the woman it didn't matter. She agreed."

Doc nodded. "They're fatalistic. A lot of folks are. It's probably the best way to be.

I try to be but I'm not too successful at it."
Doc looked around. "This is the one time
of day when the desert is beautiful and—
well—eternal with a promise that things
continue—even after death, Whit."

The cigarette was down to a nubbin so
Whit dropped it and stepped on it. "You
ready to start back?"

Doc shrugged. "Don't take him back,
Whit."

"I don't figure to. He's no good to me
dead. They'll bury him. Anyway, Deacon
got his damned money back . . . That homesteader named Thorpe . . . there's still a big
stout sorrel horse around here somewhere.
The homesteader and his boy could maybe
hire out to ride if they had an animal like
that to do it on."

Doc rubbed the tip of his nose. "That's
a good idea. In fact I know some stockmen
I can speak to." He grinned a little. "Sometimes it's good to have folks a little
beholden to you. What about the big bay he

rode down here—the horse in the corral with the old man's grey?"

"Leave it here."

Doc agreed with that. "Glad you thought of it."

Whit's gaze narrowed just a trifle. "You're sure that was just *my* idea?"

Doc smiled again. "Well, I did have a notion to suggest it." He looked past and Whit saw from his expression that someone was approaching. He turned.

Eulalia Costanso was approaching with two glasses and a greenish old bottle. She handed each of them a glass and poured the wine without looking up nor saying a word but when they were holding the full glasses and gazing at her she said, "My father says we are your host and hostess."

Doc sipped the warm wine, saw something, paused between sips to look at it more closely and then arose and strolled over near the faggot corral with his back to them.

Whit had not tasted the wine. In the growing dawn she was more beautiful than he had thought. Her features were perfectly matched, her complexion was flawless, her liquid dark eyes and ebon hair made the soft creaminess of her skin tone more nearly warm-shaded.

"*Señorita* . . . ?"

"*Señor?*"

He held the glass motionless. "We'll stay and dig the grave."

"No, *Señor.* But my father . . . and I . . . are grateful that you would have done it."

"*Señorita* . . . ?"

"*Señor?*"

"It must be ten miles to Buckeye."

"Fourteen, *Señor.*"

"You don't come up there often. I've never seen you in town."

"I've been there and I've seen you, several times."

"Well; can you come up there again . . . sometime?"

She dropped her gaze to the wine bottle she was holding. "My brother died before the sun arose."

He took that as a mild rebuke and accepted it but there was nothing for him to say which he had not already said.

"My father—"

"Sure. I understand, Eulalia." He handed her the glass and when she glanced from its scarcely touched contents to his face he smiled. "Save it. I'll be back."

". . . *Jefe?*"

He waited.

"What happens now?"

"Nothing. We recovered the money and gave it back. The other outlaw is dead. That's the end of it. Well . . . there'll be questions but it's finished anyway. Your brother . . ." He looked into her lifted face. "I've already said it once—I'm sorry. I hope your father will understand."

He turned to walk over where Doctor Nash was standing, slowly rolling a fresh cigar in his mouth. "Let's go, Doc."

He did not even mind the razor-backed harness-horse until they were almost back over to the stageroad where there was no sign of the stagecoach. No sign of anything which had occurred last night, in fact.

Then he swore and tried shifting position and Doc mentioned again stuffing sagebrush in his trousers until Whit gestured.

"Where the hell do you see any sagebrush—just show me one clump."

A mile farther along with the sun climbing and the clear air broadening their view by the minute Whit glanced back.

Doc shook his head. "You can't see anything from here."

"I've never seen her before, Doc."

"Yes, but I got the impression back there you will not let that condition prevail into the future," Nash murmured dryly. Then he slapped dust from his coat.

"Doc, you've seen her before. You've

treated her twice."

"Yes, I know." Doc looked at the ears of his horse, then above and beyond them. "Do you know how old I am?"

"No. But what's that got to do—?"

"Sixty-four, *mi amigo,* is too damned old to go through all that again. The sighing, the sleepless nights, the heartache, the inability to concentrate. Anyway, I've lived alone so long now I enjoy being that way. But good Lord—she is beautiful." He smiled a little, still looking dead ahead. "I thought of her. In fact I thought of her quite often. She's not more than thirty. Whit, a man can't give away *that* many years. Ten, yes, fifteen, maybe even twenty, but beyond that—no—and he is a fool if he thinks otherwise."

Doc fished in his pockets but there were no cigars left so he slapped his coat pockets and re-seated himself in the saddle, then said, "She is probably the most lovely woman you will ever see, Whit."

"Doc, I'm pushing forty."

"Exactly the correct age. Without a doubt the exact right age for a man to marry. Take my word for it."

Doc smiled.

They rode a long while in silence. Whit kept thinking back to the things they had said to one another. "I don't know how she did it, Doc. She knew exactly the right things to say every time."

Doc sighed. "Kick that darned horse out, will you, I need something to eat, something to drink, ten hours of sleep and a bath, a shave and two hours of sitting out back of the house in evening shade with a cigar."

12

ANOTHER DAY

People saw them enter town—that could not have been avoided—but since no one had known where they had been or why they had been down there only a few eyebrows were raised.

From the livery barn where they left Doc's horse they walked in tired silence up as far as the rear gate of Henderson's corralyard and they parted with a nod, Doc in the direction of his cottage, Turner Whitsett to pass into the corralyard where a pair of surprised yardmen looked at him, recognising the horse he was leading, without saying a word.

He tied the horse to a rail, nodded at the stationary hostlers and trudged on down to Deacon's office, dusty, unshaven and tired enough to be solemn, and when he walked in from out back and Deacon recognised him he crossed to a chair, sank down and said, "I rode a stage-horse back. It's a long story, Deacon. I boarded the southbound below town and rode it about ten, fourteen miles from town. He stopped us down there. He also rode from town—in the leather boot for baggage on the rear of the coach."

"He was on the stage all the damned time?"

Whit nodded. "Came up over the top and used a gun to stop the rig."

Deacon swore then rocked back in his squeaky old chair. "I'll be double-damned. Did he take the box?"

"Yeah."

"You got him, Whit? You brought the son of a bitch back?"

"No. He's dead." Whit was now at the place where he had to cause a diversion or explain the rest of it. He chose the diversion. With a slap on dusty trouserlegs he arose. "Send the money down, Deacon. You can have those same two swampers you had sitting in here all night ride shotgun with it. In fact, now you could send it without a guard if you were sure your driver wouldn't run off with it. Anyway, it's safe to send it now."

Deacon gazed at the standing lawman. "I always had faith in you," he said and when Whit reached the roadway door to place a hand upon the latch Henderson had something else to say. "You got 'em both. I knew you could do it, Whit."

Outside the heat was bearing down as Whit went over to the tonsorial parlour to get the key, a towel and a chunk of brown

lye-soap and head out back for the
bath-house. The water was lukewarm,
which was satisfactory because inside the
little square building it was almost as hot as
it was outside. He soaked for more than a
half hour until when he looked at his hands
they were puckered and wrinkly from sub-
mersion, then he climbed out, dried off, got
dressed and headed for the café.

Not a word was said by the caféman
beyond his customary remark about the
weather. Nor did Whit volunteer anything.
The food made a difference as he strolled
across to the jailhouse to go out back and
shave, fling the soapy water at some straggly
geraniums which seemed to thrive on that
kind of water, then to go inside, to the back
room and change into clean clothing.

Then he went to the desk, tipped back
a chair, tipped down his old hat and within
a minute was asleep.

Interruptions normally did not occur
this time of day. Buckeye during siesta-time

was like a ghost town. There was no reason for an interruption, either. Whether the town knew it or not, the matter of that stolen army payroll was over and finished with.

Even so, Whit got a two-hour respite before two men walked in bringing the coppery scent of heat with them and Whit opened one eye at a time to gaze at them from beneath the tipped down hatbrim.

One of them apologised. "It's a bad time, Marshal. We wouldn't normally bust in on a man this time of day. . . ."

Whit bit back a yawn, eased his chair down and shoved back the hat. "Mister Thorpe. . . ."

The settler smiled a little and shoved a thumb in the direction of his companion, an older man, more bent and if anything even more threadbare and destitute in appearance. "This here is Mister Cummings, Marshal. That old horse the outlaw stole belonged to him."

Whit motioned. "Seats, gents. Sit down and get comfortable." He pushed up a smile.

As they sat Thorpe spoke again, "Mister Cummings found the stout sorrel horse tied in some trees along the foothills ahind his farm, Marshal. We brought him to town with us to hand over to you."

Whit studied them briefly then had a question for the old settler. "Mister Cummings, you got your horse back?"

"Yes sir. Mister Thorpe here brung him back today." Cummings was a wiry man with coarse features, thick and heavy. His eyes were very dark in a sun-bronzed setting. He could have been almost as old as the old Mexican whose son had died before sun-up this morning. Or he could have been fifteen years younger. It was difficult to tell with those stringy, spare men.

"What I was wondering," Cummings said, "I got a huntin' hound, Marshal, that can track down anythin' with two legs, or four legs if he's put on the scent and that feller who stole my horse and then run off. . . . "

"That man is dead," stated Whit. "He was killed last night. Well! I'm not sure about the exact time, gents, but it was dark out."

The face of old Cummings fell. Clearly, he'd had some idea of hiring out his dog to track down the outlaw. Whit eased the disappointment a little by saying, "Every now and then I got need for that kind of a dog, though, Mister Cummings, and to my knowledge there's not another one around."

Cummings seemed willing to settle for this as the lawman arose to accompany them back out into the sun-smash.

The big sorrel horse was out there, tucked up but otherwise not too badly off. On each side of him was an older animal. As the men stood in overhang shade talking a slight rider appeared up the north

roadway riding Whit's second horse, the
bay.

Thorpe said, "Ulysses rode part way
down with us, Marshal, then he hung back.
I guess to ride alone the rest of the way. Just
him and your horse."

Whit looked up, watching the boy. He
was riding with a loose rein, moving in perfect unison with the bay. In a very short
time they had reached that uniquely perfect
understanding which occasionally occurs
between a horse and rider.

Cummings fidgeted, then excused himself, heading for the general store.

Whit said, "How's your missus, Mister
Thorpe?"

"She's feelin' right fit today, Marshal."
Thorpe smiled slightly. "I told her. And I
gave her that seven dollars."

Whit looked out at the big sorrel horse.
"Take him back with you, Mister Thorpe."

"What?"

"The sorrel. Take him back with you."

Whit looked around. "Maybe he's a stolen animal. Likely he is, and maybe someday someone will come looking for him. The town's not going to board him until that feller shows up or he'd eat up his worth in a few months. Take him up there, use him for his keep—maybe hire out with him. Some of the cow outfits can use a man who works hard and fetches along his own horse. But take care of him, Mister Thorpe, he's a good animal."

The homesteader stood staring. Whit ignored this to watch Ulysses come over to the rack and dismount, then to stand there forcing a smile as he looked at Marshal Whitsett.

Whit cleared his throat. "Ulysses, I got a proposition to make to you. That bay horse—I already got a horse and I don't often use the bay, so he just stands around down at the livery barn doing nothing, which isn't good for a horse . . . Your paw's going to take the big sorrel back. You can

have that bay horse. The pair of you can
hire out." He shrugged at the expression of
stunned rapture on the boy's face. "Treat
him good, Ulysses. He's gentle and willing
and as honest as the day is long." Whit shot
a squinty-eyed glance upward. "Well, gents,
it's about time for me to make my rounds."
As he turned to depart he said, "Mister
Thorpe—the very next time your wife has
one of her spells you fetch her down here to
Doc Nash. All right?"

"I promise, Marshal. But about—"

"Forget about it, Mister Thorpe. But if
a man ever rides in like that again, you send
for me right off."

Whit walked northward without
looking back, crossed up in the direction of
the saloon and walked in where Will Austen
was polishing glasses in a temperature
which had to be at least ten degrees cooler
than it was outside.

Will nodded. He did not know the town
marshal had not been in Buckeye since the

day before, or at least the night before, nor did he know that second outlaw had been killed and as they leaned to talk in the pleasant gloom Whit did not tell him. All he discussed was the possibility of a summer thundershower and true to his temperament Austen curled his lips and scorned any such idea.

"It ain't done it but once since I been down here," he exclaimed in a voice of unimpeachable authority, "and it ain't goin' to do it this summer." Then Will said, "Any new developments about that danged outlaw you didn't find, Whit?"

The marshal smiled. "I came in for a glass of beer."

Austen went to fill a glass dutifully and return with it. Then he stood expectantly silent while Whit drank half the tepid brew and afterwards dug out his makings to go to work over a cigarette.

"Deacon got the money back, the few other little details of that matter got cleaned up, Will, and if you got a match I can smoke along with my beer, which seems to me to be about what a man's got a right to do on a day as hot as this one is."

Austen did not return to the subject. He acted as though he were satisfied, as though perhaps his curiosity had not been inordinately large in the first place. Nor was it, about this matter nor any other matter once the source for suspicion and derogation had gone out of things. Will was one of those people who throve only on other people's shortcomings and between periods when these inevitably surfaced he bided his time and was not very interested.

But his beer was not the worst Whit had ever tasted, and his ancient adobe bar-building with its three-foot thick mud walls was about the coolest place in town this time of year, and made Austen's company bearable. The alternative was one of the three Mex *cantinas* over along the east side of Buckeye with their equally thick walls, their dirt floors and *cerbeza* which tasted like beer only after a drinker had filtered out the floating bits of ancient wood and occasionally dead flies which could be stopped from entering a drinker's mouth providing he held his teeth just so as he sipped.

There were a lot of imperfections on the south desert and in Buckeye at times it had seemed to Marshal Whitsett over the years they congregated this time of year, or a little earlier, right close to town. But as the summer advanced, as the heat gradually climbed until even lizards panted in the shade, trouble of all kinds seemed to diminish and for that reason alone Turner Whitsett was never too disparaging about summertime.

He left Austen's bar and went up to his room at the boarding-house to lie down and rest away what was left of siesta-time, perfectly confident there would be no trouble. It was getting too hot for a man to hold a gunbarrel.

13

AFTERMATH

Deacon of course told Will Austen that the second outlaw had stowed away on the stagecoach. He also told him this man had been killed in a gunfight ten or so miles below town, so when Whit entered the saloon before supper with darkness over the south desert Will was waiting to reproach him for being secretive earlier in the day and Whit smiled, called for another glass of tepid beer and leaned there feeling more relaxed and comfortable than he had felt in several days.

Except for his rear.

When Austen re-told things as he had got them from Deacon Henderson Whit nodded his head and sipped beer and when Austen was beginning to get a little pink in the face Whit said, "You know as much about it as anyone does, Will. The outlaws are both dead, the money was recovered. That ends it."

Austen wanted details. "How did the fight start?" he asked. "Was you alone down there?"

Will was considering his answer when a pair of big, sweaty freighters, bearded and brawny and testy-looking, barged in and growled for beer so Will had to depart. While he was up there taking care of his new customers one of the freighters loudly proclaimed Buckeye to be the hottest, most inconsequential, least inviting town he had ever visited and Will Austen arose to the defence.

Whit chuckled to himself and left.

Doc was over in front of the harness works so Whit strolled down and crossed over. Doc was fresh and clean, but his gaze was sardonic. "This damned town," he said. "A man could shoot a cannon right down through town at siesta-time and except for me no one would even hear it."

"Why except for you?"

"Did you give that squatter kid your bay horse?"

"Yeah. I didn't ride him enough to pay for his keep. What of it?"

"That darned little devil woke me up by banging on the back door. He wanted me to look at a brush scratch the horse had got the last day or two on his front left leg. Whit, I've got worse scratches than that and didn't even know it. Why the hell do people always think of me when they get some silly little thing—?"

"Doc, maybe when you were a kid you had something to cotton to; a dog or a cat or maybe a horse. It fills a need in a kid's life to be responsible for something. He thinks the sun rises and sets on that bay horse." Whit shoved a hand into a trouser pocket. "How much does he owe you?"

Doc grimaced. "Who ever heard of charging a kid," he grumbled and stood a moment looking at his friend before also saying, "Hell, I guess if you can give the kid a horse I can doctor him now and then for no charge." Doc sighed. "Only I hope after this he doesn't show up down here when I'm worn out and trying to get some rest."

"I told his paw to keep the sorrel too. If someone comes along someday to claim him, well, we'll worry about that when it happens. I also told him to fetch his missus to see you the very next time she don't feel well. Knowing those people—he'll probably arrive in town when we're takin' our afternoon naps, too."

Doctor Nash showed resignation. "I wish to hell they'd adapt."

"Give 'em time, Doc. They're not

Mexes; it takes all of us a little time to get used to sleeping in the afternoon." Whit looked up and down the empty roadway. "I haven't told anyone how that feller died down south and I haven't mentioned his name or where we left him."

Doc understood. "They'll play hell getting anything out of me. Will Austen included . . . How about Deacon and the money?"

Whit was not very interested. "I told him it's safe to send it along to Coldspring. I expect he'll do it, maybe on tonight's coach. Otherwise he's going to have some mad soldiers looking him up for their payroll. He said something, though, that makes sense; let the company either provide an armed escort or let the army provide it or else send those darned money-pouches by way of Lordsburg or some other route south." Whit saw those two big freighters emerge from the saloon heading for the café and asked if Doc had had supper.

He hadn't so they both struck out across the road in the same direction those freighters had taken.

The evening arrived as it usually did, quietly and without any great flare of dying sunlight. It just came softly and quietly with the same ancient sequence it had always followed on the south desert, making thoughtful people reflect upon the endlessness of time and their minuscule part in it.

Whit locked up early and bedded down for a full night's sleep eventually with a reasonably clear conscience; he was not a youth and therefore it was impossible for him to lie in the cool darkness as many did, momentarily reviewing their lives or at least their most recent activities, with complete satisfaction.

He should not have left that dead outlaw down there, for one thing, and he had no real authority to give away that sorrel horse. Nor was he legally entitled to cover up how that second outlaw had died or who had shot him.

But Buckeye was not New York or even Denver, it was as removed from those cities as was the moon. Its lawman was and always had been more than just an enforcer of the law. It did not have to be right, any of it, it just had to work to keep the community safe and peaceful, and that is what it did—that is what *he* did.

When he finally slept it was without a dream or a noise or any kind of interruption so maybe the shades of conscience which would have troubled purists, sticklers for the letter of the law, were not too well developed in him.

He awakened the same way, without a troubling thought.

Reb Hunter the liveryman nodded at the door of the café as he and Whit met down there and entered to the aroma of frying eggs and meat. Old Reb asked about the bay horse. All Whit said was, "I gave him away," and at the old man's surprised attention, he said, "Why should I pay you to board him and never use him?"

Reb watched his breakfast platter arrive and considered its handsome array of fried eggs and steak swimming in grease and said, "I'd have given you fifteen dollars for him."

Whit abandoned the topic and ate. He was hungry, which he normally was not this early in the morning and his rear still felt sensitive every time he sat down. Well, after an interlude of dealing with two deadly out-laws, stolen money and a gunfight a man had a right to feel bad *somewhere* but that was not normally the place a man expected to feel that way.

Across the road at the jailhouse there were two letters waiting, shoved under the door by one of the yardmen from Deacon's place. One was from the commanding colonel at Fort Hannibal. It was sarcastic and derogatory. The other letter was from Henderson's employers who owned the stage company, and while its purpose was to ask for details of the robbery, it had some uncomplimentary suggestions to make also.

He tossed them both in a little box he kept handy for paper and kindling for the stove and walked out into the magnificent cool morning.

An old Mexican wood-gatherer named Esteben was trudging by, his undersized burro nearly hidden beneath a load of faggots.

Whit said, *"Buenas dias, amigo."*

The wizened, leathery-faced old man turned friendly, shrewd dark eyes when he replied in slurred Spanish. Esteben had so few teeth even in anger his words were not distinct.

"Buenas dias, jefe," he responded and paused with a hand held back for the burro to halt also. The little animal turned soulful eyes towards Turner Whitsett and patiently waited as his owner said in the same slurred border-Spanish, "A man defends the things

he believes in. You must never feel badly."

Then the old man smiled and clucked at the burro to go shuffling along.

Whit lit a smoke wondering what that had meant. He was ready to walk up to Deacon's office to ascertain if the Coldspring payroll had gone south when an idea came and he stood a moment in deep shade smoking and looking up where the old Mexican was turning eastward from the main roadway heading for Mex-town.

Then he shrugged it off and walked up to listen to Deacon's profanity out back in the corralyard where a greenhorn swamper had hooked check-reins on the horses being hitched to the morning coach.

"You bloody simpleton, this ain't Denver. It ain't even Lordsburg. We don't use check-reins on the desert. Who cares whether horses go out of Buckeye with their heads up or not! What we want is honest service not no gawd-damned show-off silliness. Now take off them check-reins and for all I care you can pitch them in the manure pile!"

The red-faced hostler used both hands to fumble in all haste at the harness as Whit dropped his smoke and stepped on it as Deacon turned on him, still furious. Whit smiled a little. "Nice to know you're back to just being a bully instead of worrying about money-pouches."

"I'm not no damned bully but by golly when they commence using check-reins down here . . ." Deacon came down off his peak of anger slowly. "Is somethin' wrong?"

"Not that I know of. Did you get rid of that payroll?"

Deacon looked left and right, then dropped his voice. "Sent it out last night with them two swampers riding inside the coach with scatterguns."

"Then it ought to be down at Cold-spring some time this morning. That's all I wanted to know. Now go back to picking on your hired help."

Whit turned to stroll back to the roadway but Deacon caught up and again protested that he was not being hard on his men. Whit said, "Go tell that to the kid back there," and was half way across the road before a thought struck him hard.

That old Mex wood-gatherer . . . He changed course, headed down through the dog-trot between Austen's saloon and the building next to it and emerged into Mex-town with its haphazardly placed little adobe houses, its raffish mongrel dogs, all thin, all probably wormy, and its crooked little narrow dusty pathways.

Even the smell down here was different. The people ate spiced, highly seasoned foods. They cooked differently too but it was a rather pleasant fragrance as he went trudging northward in the direction of the mud cubicle where the faggot-gatherer lived.

Esteben was out back, hatless now, old baggy shirt and trousers sagging from a thin, wiry frame, feeding tortillas to the soulful-eyed little burro who was eating the tortillas the way a horse would eat hay, as though he enjoyed them. They were not made of corn the way tortillas were made in better-endowed countrysides. Down on the south desert no one raised corn, not because it would not grow there but because there was no way to water the rows, so the tortillas were made from lumpy flour.

The burro saw Whit first and pushed over-sized ears forward as he thoughtfully masticated. Old Esteben turned, looked surprised at the identity of his visitor, then put the remaining tortillas on the ground so the burro could eat by himself, wiped worn old hands on his trouser-legs and made a toothless wide smile.

"*Jefe.* . . ."

Whit offered tobacco, a luxury, and the old man immediately worked dark fingers like the legs of a spider twisting up a cigarette. Whit held the match, then said, "What did I defend that I believed in, *viego?*"

Esteben held his smoke with the cultivated casualness of someone accustomed to such luxuries and looked up. "What happened to Adolfo Costanso's son, *jefe.*"

This was the root of that thought which had struck Whit back up town. "What happened—just happened, *viego.* I was not the one who shot him. But—how did you know?"

Esteben was thoroughly enjoying this. He was scorned even by his neighbours. He was an old man long past usefulness except as a gatherer of dry wood, faggots, which he sold as firewood for the stoves around town. It gave him barely as many copper coins as were required for him to keep body and soul together and also the body and soul of his little burro. To be called upon by someone as exalted as the town marshal, to know something this exalted individual, this handsome *gringo* of formidable authority, did not know, made him feel even better.

He shrugged thin old shoulders, determined to extract every moment of superiority from this interlude. "A man hears things, *jefe*, from the birds, even, and the little desert foxes and the—"

"And the burros, you old devil, and the *garropatos* waiting on bush-limbs to drop on people," replied Whit in border-Spanish. "When you are finished, I will appreciate an honest answer."

That was the wrong word. Old Esteben's shoulders squared, his ancient face of dark parchment turned mildly affronted. "I am a man of honour," he said. "I have lived all my life as a man of—"

"Keep the tobacco sack, old friend of great honour. Just answer me. How did you know?"

"Does it matter?" replied the old man, instantly stuffing the little cloth sack of tobacco into the folds of his old shirt.

Whit sighed to himself. "It matters, old friend, if as I believe the source of this information was someone—else."

Esteben's eyes drew out narrow in their knowing shrewdness. "Do you know the Aguirres, *jefe?*"

Whit knew them; they had nine children of which four were boys, young men who worked as tophands for local cow outfits. "Yes. What of them?"

"They are old friends of Adolfo Costanso."

Whit waited, hoping he was correct in what he was thinking. "What of that, old one?"

Esteben was nearing the end of his moment of triumph and had to face it. He inhaled, exhaled, and said, "The Aguirres are old friends of that old *Gachupíne* who lives down near the border with his goats."

"Adolfo Costanso."

"*Sí*, Adolfo Costanso."

It was like pulling teeth. "What of that,

old friend?"

"They are over at the Aguirre's house."

"They?"

"The old man and his daughter, *jefe.*"

Whit and the old man looked steadily at one another over an interval of silence, then Whit asked when the Costansos had arrived and Esteben made a little gesture of uncertainty when he replied.

"I think it was last night, late, after the darkness."

"And you saw them, then?"

"Yes. I was down at the cantina and saw them come into town from the southeast. I did not know—was not sure—at first. The old man was riding a fine bay horse."

Old Esteben might have been old and frail and useless in many ways, but his mind was fully alive. He gazed at the taller younger man for a moment then said, "You did right, *jefe.* A bad man like that is—well—may the priest forgive me for saying it but he is a man of no worth. A *pistolero* of

no honour. It is better for this world that he
is no longer in it."

"I didn't shoot him, Esteben. If you're
trying to make me feel better."

The old man's eyes narrowed again
showing doubt, but he was tactful, which
was one thing an old man learned to be
since he was no longer *macho* enough to
defend himself. "However it is, chief," he
murmured in that slurred way of speaking,
"the thing is done and it was something
which was supposed to happen. The only
thing, even for that kind of *bastardo*, is for
people to hope death came swiftly and he
died in His Grace."

Whit smiled. "I still didn't kill him,
amigo." He turned to depart and the old
man had one more thing to say.

"*Jefe*, you must learn to like goats."
Then he cackled as Whit walked away.

14

THE PLAZA

The Aguirre adobe was on the east side of Mex-town with the rear of the house to the open desert. Someone generations earlier had planted trees beyond the house; cottonwoods, crab-apples and three citrus trees which bore pithy fruit because neglect went with the years and changing ownership and the feeling people had, different from the original planters. But the shade was more to be savoured than the fruit anyway.

Whit knew the family, had visited with Rudolfo the paunchy, good-natured patriarch many times. When he came down through the dust this morning the old man recognised him. He could perhaps have anticipated this visit, even so early in the day. The way news travelled throughout Mex-town (*huaracha* telegraph, the sanguine *gringos* called it, referring to the leather sandals—*huarachas*—worn by *peon* Mexicans) these people knew of events often before the *gringos* did.

The older man leaned upon a juniper upright which supported the overhang-roof—called a *ramada*—out front of his house, light coppery face with good features settled in an expression of almost sad pensiveness. When Whit came up and smiled the heavy older man smiled and gallantly gestured to a chair with sagging rawhide bottom. In good English he said, "Pleasures begin at sun-up and end at high noon," then he chuckled and went to take one of the chairs himself. He sat and waited, a heavy man who had once been physically powerful and tireless and who now in his sun-down years no longer worried about the first thing to foresake strong men—their muscles.

Whit would have offered tobacco but old Esteben had got that a half hour before so he said, "The boys are working, Rudolfo?"

"Yes, Marshal, they all four went to work for the Pothook cow outfit this season. It is the first time all four have ever worked at the same time for one brand."

"They are tophands," stated Whit, and Rudolfo nodded with gentle pride.

"They are honest men, *jefe*. I have reason to be satisfied."

"Any marriages near?"

Rudolfo laughed. "Well, *mi mujer* and I have hopes. But girls are secretive." Rudolfo rolled up his eyes. "So secretive all the time." He suddenly looked steadily at

Whit. "And you, old friend . . . ?"

Whit reddened without any idea it was going to happen. "Marriage . . . me?"

Rudolfo spread big hands, palms up. "Who am I to advise the *jefe* of the township. . . ."

Whit fidgeted. In Spanish he said, "You are an old, valued friend. Anything you have to say, companion, I will value."

Rudolfo eased back in his chair. From out back someone was berating chickens in Spanish for getting into a garden patch and several doors southward in another adobe house a baby's thin wail rose and fell, then rose again.

Rudolfo was waiting again. Whit shifted in the chair again, partly from self-consciousness, partly because his rear was tender.

"You have house guests, then?" he asked in Spanish.

Rudolfo showed no surprise at all. "My cousin," he said simply, surprising Whit,

who had had no idea there was a relation-
ship.

Aguirre watched the lawman a
moment. "They told us," he said without
elaborating. "There was no surprise. They
have been expecting it for several years. I
think it was a relief. It is over. Of course
there is grief but it will eventually die. The
other thing, the anxiety, the dread, the tor-
ment, would have remained as long as the
son of my cousin lived. This way—now it is
over."

Whit looked up. "Is that how the old
man feels?"

Aguirre nodded and raised his eyes as
someone appeared in the doorway behind
Whit to his left. Whit turned.

She was wearing one of those loose,
short-sleeved full blouses with embroidery
on the yoke and around the scoop of the
throat and a fawn-coloured long skirt. Her
hair was shiny in its ebon darkness, making
a black contrast for her golden skin and her

flawless face.

He arose and old Rudolfo also struggled upright although he probably would not have if the marshal hadn't. Rudolfo sighed and muttered something about those chickens around back and went shuffling around the side of the house.

Whit said, "I sure hoped you wouldn't wait too long."

She remained in the dark doorway looking at him, her strong chin and jaw rounded, her full, handsome mouth slightly tough-set. "My father wanted to leave for a few days," she told him. "So did I."

He groped for something to say. "Well; it's pleasant these mornings."

She moved, went over to the chair her uncle had vacated and stood a moment before seating herself. "How did you know, *jefe?*"

"An old friend told me."

She faced him. "Really? A spy then?"

"No, not a spy. Just a friend who saw

you and your father ride in last night. I
don't spy on people." He hid the mild
annoyance with a little smile at her.
"There's enough trouble around without
looking for more."

She continued to watch his face, his
expressions, his eyes. She said, "Have you
ever seen a Mexican play?"

He hadn't but he knew when troupes
arrived from Mexico two or three times a
year to give their presentations. A lot of
people came over to watch but he never
had. For no real reason, except that he'd
just never felt the urge.

"I never have," he admitted. "Is there
one coming?"

"It is here. They will act tonight at the
plaza."

He met her honest gaze—with red
beginning to rise. "Well; would it be all
right if I came over and we went together?"

She was solemn when she nodded her
head. "I think it would be very nice, *jefe.*"

"What time tonight?"

"Eight o'clock. You can come here or I can be on the benches at the plaza."

He did not like the idea of meeting her so he said, "Here, at eight o'clock."

They continued to sit for a while. He mentioned how dry it was this summer and she gave the standard answer to that. If they did not get early rains this autumn the wells might go dry.

He left with the sun heading towards its zenith, aware that a number of people from other houses around and those passing by the house from out front had looked in surprise, then quick interest, at him sitting out there with her.

When he got back over to the jailhouse there was a dusty cavalry lieutenant sitting out front under the overhang smoking a long cigar, waiting. He was a lanky, greying, hard-faced man with a slight Southern accent and deep-set, observant eyes. Whit took him inside where it was much cooler

and offered the *olla*. The lieutenant drank,
sat down and trickled fragrant smoke as he
asked about the robbery. He already knew
from Will Austen at the bar that the money
had been recovered and no doubt that had
something to do with his attitude. He was
one of those spare, easy-moving men whose
temperament slid between yeastiness and
quiet amiability. Whit thought it was a good
thing the lieutenant already knew the Coldspring payroll had been recovered. The soldier was a man accustomed to authority; to
be being blunt. Now he listened to all Whit
had to say and asked only one question.

"The outlaws are both dead?"

"Yes. And Mister Henderson at the
depot sent the payroll down to Coldspring
last night. By now they've got it."

The lieutenant relaxed and considered
his cigar. "I'm glad, Marshal." He raised his
clear, direct gaze. "The commanding
officer at Hannibal is disagreeable about
things like this."

Whit caught the implication easily enough and gave the soldier look for look. "Lieutenant, if you want to make sure your money gets through send an armed escort with it. I'm one man without any deputies. I don't like having someone dump that kind of responsibility on me without warning. Next time maybe I won't be so lucky and you'll never recover the money."

The officer fell to considering his cigar again, more meticulously and thoughtfully this time. "Marshal, the War Department has us cut back until we can't even replace over-age horses. The colonel wouldn't want to send an escort."

Whit answered that curtly. "Then take the risk, Lieutenant."

The officer smoked a moment in silence. "Folks around Buckeye have worlds of faith in you, Marshal. The man at the stage office, the barman, the liveryman, the storekeeper across the road . . ." He blew a bluish cloud at the fly-specked ceiling, then brought his eyes down, smiling. "So have I." He arose. "I'm right obliged for your time, Marshal."

Whit watched the door open and close, then groped through a drawer until he found an unopened sack of tobacco and rolled a smoke.

The heat was rising and the town was gradually getting quiet the way it usually did as the morning advanced. He went up to the tonsorial parlour, got a chunk of lye soap, a towel and the key to the bathhouse. The barber turned and watched him go out the back door and when Doc Nash ambled in a few minutes later to be shaved and shorn the barber said, "Doc, if a man takes a bath two days in a row, it ain't healthy is it?"

Doc sat down and rolled his collar under. "Who?"

"The marshal."

Doc finished with the collar. "Turner Whitsett?"

"Yeah. Yesterday, and now he's out

there again."

Doc sat a moment in thought. "Does seem odd, but it won't hurt a person. Leave off that French toilet water, Sam. I don't want to walk out of here smelling like a dance-hall."

They did not meet. Doc was gone by the time Whit brought back the soap and soggy towel and went on up to his room at the boarding-house.

The day ended slowly. There was one minor flurry of excitement. The northbound driver did not cut wide enough when he turned into the corralyard and hooked a rear hub on a gatepost. Deacon came boiling out of his office, green eyeshade askew, to curse and stamp and shake his fist. The driver sat up there looking down for a moment, then methodically set the binders, looped his lines, climbed slowly down, turned and hit Deacon so hard that Henderson bounced off the frayed gatepost and slid down into an unconscious, inert lump.

The swampers stood in frozen astonishment while the driver removed his
gauntlets, eyed Deacon with no show of
emotion, then shoved the big gloves under
his belt and sauntered over to the saloon.

By the time Whit came back down
through on his way to the café for supper
the story was all over town. He did not hear
it until he was at the counter and the
caféman told him. He was not particularly
interested, not even when Deacon came in
a little later while Whit was finishing supper
and sat down, showing a swollen and dis-
coloured jaw and cheek.

He glared when the caféman murmured something which Whit did not make
out, then turned and also met the lawman's
gaze of mild interest. "I bumped into a
post," he snarled.

Whit accepted that and went back to
drinking coffee. When he finished he paid
up, gave Deacon a slight pat on the

shoulder and said, "I knew it was going to happen, Deacon. If it wasn't that young hostler the other day over the check-reins, then something else."

He walked on out into the lowering dusk and could smell cook-stove wood-smoke out over town. He had an hour to kill so he made a round of Buckeye, then locked the jailhouse for the night, examined his coat for dust or lint, polished each boot-toe upon a trouser-leg and went out back to Mex-town where there was a subdued feeling of excitement. People were strolling toward the plaza in their best attire, children with black eyes almost as large as saucers, young *vaqueros* with their spurs out a notch so they would ring with each boot-step, lovely girls with creamy shoulders and masses of black hair piled high. And there was the fragrance of tortillas, of candied squash and of a particular festive food which *gringos* were just beginning to adopt—popped corn.

He braced himself for the stares of all the Aguirres and walked over to the house. They were gone, had left a half hour earlier, Eulalia told him as she arose from a chair out front at his approach. She smiled in the shadows. "I thought it would be easier for you. . . . The play began at seven-thirty."

He laughed with her. She had a pale blue *rebozo,* a dark blouse and a leather belt at her waist with a silver filagree buckle. She was beautiful. He told her so, then took her hand.

She was silent at his side. He was very conscious of her each time they brushed or touched.

The plaza of Mex-town was a large, dusty, circular area with an ancient well in the centre. This had originally been the town and it had been called in Spanish The City Of Our Lady Of the Agonies; but that was not only too long, it was also a tongue-twister in Spanish, so the newcomers had named the place Buckeye for no particular reason that anyone could recall now.

For benches there were cottonwood logs rolled out and placed one behind the other. For lights there were dozens of smoking candles in front of the place where the players had unrolled their threadbare old green groundcloth.

Whit sat beside Eulalia Costanso, hat in his lap, while a stooped, evil man with a very long nose of paste and a forked beard leered and attempted to paw a buxom woman of about forty but made up to look like a virgin of sixteen. The heavily made-up woman rolled her eyes to heaven, heaved a bosom no girl of sixteen could have possibly possessed and ground her teeth in an agony of despair either because she liked what the evil man was doing or was at least attempting to do or maybe because he was driving her to a prayer to God to save her from his clutches.

Whit watched impassively until he felt the beautiful woman beside him turning to look, then he turned and slowly winked. She looked as though she would laugh, but just fleetingly, then turned back and became properly concerned for the 'girl's' imperilled virtue. Around them dozens of people who had never seen Eulalia Costanso and who had never before seen Marshal Whitsett at a play in Mex-town were divided in their interest.

The imperilled virgin was suddenly saved when a brave lieutenant of Santa Anna's National Guard complete with great, curved sabre which dragged at his heels, high jack-boots and magnificent gold-braided jacket and trousers strode forth to lay a hand upon the hilt of his sword with a grand flourish.

Whit knew at once the 'girl' was to be saved. But he had never seen one of these plays before. The evil man with the forked Spanish beard whipped out a pistol and shot the brave lieutenant dead. The lieutenant first showed astonishment, then he looked at the blood on his hand, which miraculously had not stained the front of his elegant coat, then he looked at the 'girl', looked at the crowd, looked toward heaven, looked again at the 'girl', who sprang up and hurled herself at him. Then, finally, he fell with a great groan.

The audience properly hissed and called imprecations as the evil man pulled the 'girl' to her feet and dragged her from the stage into a clump of artificial under-brush, leering every step of the way.

The audience called and cried out and shook fists. Whit turned and saw Eulalia looking at him. He leaned a little. "Is that the end?"

She smiled. "Yes."

"But . . . but that man with the long nose was the villain."

"Yes."

"And the lieutenant . . . ?"

"The hero, *jefe.*"

They arose to stroll the bland starbright

night as dozens of other couples were doing. He finally said, "Was it supposed to end with the villain making off with the girl?"

She turned laughing dark eyes to him. "Yes. You've never seen a Mexican play before. *Jefe*, isn't that how it is in life as often as not? Maybe even oftener than not?"

He thought about that. "Maybe. But it's not supposed to be like that in plays. That lieutenant was supposed to run him through with that big sword."

She laughed. They were nearing the upper end of Mex-town where there was cooling desert and long tree-shadows from both sides of the narrow little roadway to indicate a boundary beyond which lay the ancient and eternal emptiness of a barren, sparse territory.

She said, "Did you know people stared at you?"

"Why should they stare at me? They see

me almost any day of the year. It was you they stared at."

"You were with a Mexican."

It was like a light slap. He knew what he *wanted* to say and he also knew better than to say it. "I was with a beautiful *woman*. Any place I've ever been that's what they would have stared about."

"*Jefe*, you know better than that."

He stopped and turned. "I'm not trying to be gallant, just truthful."

She met his gaze. She had a way of doing that with a look of serenity, of real confidence and calmness. "*Jefe*, I think you are a very nice man. A fine man. Different from many other men. . . . And I am a Mexican woman."

He took her by the hand and they walked on past the last adobe *jacal*, out where even the smell of goats and cooking did not reach, then they halted and looked back. She said, "You see; two separate communities."

LAURAN PAINE

He was bothered by something. "Why are you trying to make a barrier between us?"

"Because one exists, *jefe.*"

He shook his head at her slowly. "Not here," he touched the middle of his shirt-front. "Is there?"

She hung fire for a moment, unable to answer this as handily as she had answered the other statements. She looked back down toward the town. Profiled to him, she was solid and abundant and magnificent. She had a sweep from shoulders to throat which was flawless, and her mouth was strong but sensitive and sweet.

He said, "Is there?"

"No, not—here—not in the heart but in many other ways."

"Do you want me to re-make the world, Eulalia?"

"It can't be done, *jefe.*"

"You are wrong. It *can* be done. In one household at a time."

He was still holding her hand. She freed it and turned to gaze northward up over the endless bland desert and the soft night.

"I don't know," she murmured, more it seemed to herself than to him.

"No one would know unless someone just once made the effort, Eulalia . . . Would you try?"

She nodded, still not looking at him, then she turned. "Yes, I would try."

Her abrupt aquiescence pushed him off balance. She was looking at him in that very honest, serene way again. He did what he unconsciously did quite often in moments of uncertainty; he lifted his hat and re-set it atop his head without being aware he had done it even when they turned to stroll back when she told him it was required, that in Mex-town there were very strict rules governing how long young men and young women could be abroad at night without chaperones.

They got almost back to the plaza, dark

now, all those candles snuffed out, all the cottonwood-log seats empty, the artificial shrubbery and the worn green groundcloth all that remained of the play, its participants and spectators, before they saw anyone. Another couple were down there, a tall lean *vaquero* and a slip of a dark-haired girl standing together in night-shadows, whispering.

Whit watched them briefly, then shook his head and leaned to say, "I can't even remember when I was his age."

She made a little sound of disbelief, then turned him by the hand in the easterly direction of the Aguirre adobe.

When they saw the candle in the window he said, "Tomorrow evening?"

"Even if people talk?"

"Even if they scream at the top of their voices in both languages."

He swung her gently half around out front of that lighted window. "Thank you."

She smiled and again freed her fingers.

"It was very nice, *jefe.*"

"Do you know my name?"

"Yes. Turner Whitsett . . . Whit?"

"Tomorrow night, Eulalia?"

"Tomorrow night . . . Whit."

She turned and entered the house. He waited until the candle was put out then walked slowly back through the silent pathways of Mex-town back to his own part of Buckeye.

Doc Nash was leaning out front of the saloon smoking a cigar and watched as the lawman came shuffling up, lost in private thoughts. Doc removed the cigar and said, "The lieutenant should have run that other feller right through the gizzard."

"You were over there too?"

"Sure. Most everyone was . . . She is beautiful, Whit. I was just leaning here smoking and wondering what could have happened twenty, thirty years ago if I'd seen someone like her." Doc flicked ash. "I know the answer. I'd be pushing pills about as I'm doing now, but with probably ten kids and a big fat paunch . . . and with a woman to look at with beautiful eyes and a wonderful smile and . . . Hell, it's past my bedtime. Good night."

Doc stepped down into the dust and went walking in the direction of his dark residence.

Whit watched him a moment, then considered entering Will's saloon for a nightcap, decided against it for no real reason and went on slowly up to the boarding-house to turn in.

It had been a long week, a troubled week, and it had ended in a way he never would have believed it could have ended. Doc was right; she was beautiful.

Center Point Publishing
600 Brooks Road 1 PO Box 1
Thorndike ME 04986-0001 USA

(207) 568-3717

US & Canada:
1 800 929-9108